A Man Who Knows

EMMANUEL BOVE

A MAN

WHO KNOWS

Translated from the French by Janet Louth

THE MARLBORO PRESS / NORTHWESTERN

EVANSTON, ILLINOIS

The Marlboro Press/Northwestern
Northwestern University Press
Evanston, Illinois 60208-4210

Originally published in French under the title *Un homme qui savait*.
Copyright © 1985 by Editions de la Table Ronde, Paris. English translation
copyright © 1989 by Janet Louth. The Marlboro Press/Northwestern edition
published 1999 by arrangement with Carcanet Press Limited, Manchester.
All rights reserved.

Printed in the United States of America

ISBN 0-8101-6057-9

Library of Congress Cataloging-in-Publication Data

Bove, Emmanuel, 1898–
    [Homme qui savait. English]
    A man who knows / Emmanuel Bove ; translated from the French by
Janet Louth.
        p. cm.
    ISBN 0-8101-6057-9 (pbk. : alk. paper)
    I. Louth, Janet. II. Title
PQ2603.O87H6513 1999
843'.912—dc21   99-14136
                                                                       CIP

The paper used in this publication meets the minimum requirements of the
American National Standard for Information Sciences—Permanence of Paper
for Printed Library Materials, ANSI Z39.48-1984.

It was ten o'clock in the morning. Maurice Lesca picked up the oil-cloth bag, folded it and put it under his arm. He closed the door of the small kitchen. He was a man of fifty-seven who, throughout his life, had found his great height and strength more of an embarrassment than an advantage. He had as many white hairs as brown. Sometimes the light showed up one colour more, sometimes the other, making him appear older or younger. His face bore the marks of the disappointments of an already long life. He wore a battered old hat, pulled down not only over his eyes but over his ears and the back of his neck too. His grey-green overcoat was baggy. When Maurice Lesca walked down the street he could be recognized from a distance by the way he used to put his hands through the vertical opening of the pockets and hold them in front of him, as if he was hiding something too big to go into a pocket. So that no one should notice that he had neither collar nor tie, he wore a scarf crossed over his chest. His trousers were too long and covered his heels. His worn-out shoes had lost their shape and did not even quite match any longer.

'I'm going shopping,' he said to his sister, who had been living in the flat's other room for seven months.

There was no answer. It did not surprise him and he went out. He set off down the four damp storeys of the house in the rue de Rivoli, opposite the Samaritaine, where he had settled seventeen years earlier. He crossed the second-floor landing on tip-toe. There, behind a door, a dog which was left alone all day would begin to whine as soon as it heard footsteps. Maurice Lesca could not bear it. In front of the concierge's lodge he stopped for a moment to look at the letters which had been slipped between the glass and the curtain on the door. In spite of the rain, a fine invisible rain, it was crowded outside. He stayed hesitating under the porch. Usually he looked to see what kind of weather it was before he went out. That morning he had forgotten. 'That's what comes of thinking about the same thing all the time.' He went quickly past the houses to the corner of a narrow street where there was a small café. He had a drink at the bar, lit a cigarette, exchanged a few words with the owner and then left. A few moments later he half-opened the door of a laundry and, without going in, asked if his washing was ready. He was told it was and said he would collect it on his way back. Then he went to buy a few things for his lunch. In each shop he waited patiently for his turn. The shopkeeper had to speak to him before he would ask for what he wanted. For seventeen years, among the housewives of the district, he had been behaving like a newcomer who did not wish to be accused of wanting to jump the queue. In a newsagent's tiny shop a child was crying. He could be seen sitting on the floor amidst torn paper, in the airless back part of the shop.

'What's the matter? Whatever is the matter?' asked Lesca, trying to distract the child with his gestures.

The child stopped crying. His mother picked him up.

'Shake hands with the doctor.'

Lesca smiled.

He went out almost at once. It pained him to see children shut up like that. Slowly he climbed up the four storeys again. He stopped at each landing because of his heart. At last he arrived home. He put his bag in the kitchen. Then he went back into his room and sat down in a big old-fashioned leather armchair with turned feet and casters. All the furniture was of the same sort as this armchair. Seventeen years before, when he happened to be out for a walk, he had said to a small dealer in second-hand goods: 'Find me something to furnish two rooms with.' A few days later the dealer had said to him: 'I've got what you need.' Lesca had never been one to put himself out. 'I'm sure it will do perfectly. Have it all sent round to me.'

He held an unfolded newspaper in his hand. He had not taken off his overcoat or his hat. From time to time he looked out. Each time it seemed to him that the rain had stopped, but then he noticed that it was coming down more steadily than ever.

After a little while he said to his sister:

'Emily, I'm back.'

There was no reply, even though the door of the other room was open. The buses made the windows rattle. The flat had not been aired. They never aired it. The air which made its way through the window frames was enough to produce a sensation of freshness when they came back in the evening. Lesca pinched his nostrils, then he left his fingers under his nose. He liked the smell of tobacco mixed with the smell of skin. Suddenly he stood up and took off his overcoat and hat. He had not yet washed and felt ugly and dirty. He began to pace up and down. For several months he had not looked into the room now occupied by his sister. When he was tired of walking round and round, he went and sat down at a desk which stood in one corner of the room. Everything that surrounded him was grandiose and displeasing, the solid oak sideboard, the chest in a corner, the carved bedstead behind a door, the dining-room table with rounded corners, and above all the desk, covered with dusty odds and ends, with its frightful drawer at the side, divided into compartments for cash, for it was more of a counter than a desk! For some minutes his eyes rested on the massive inkstand, a small-scale brass copy of a fountain in Dijon. Then he stood up and began to walk about again.

'Emily.'

Again there was no reply. He sat down in the leather armchair once more. 'This is a fine bit of old-fashioned furniture too,' he murmured. He lit a fresh cigarette and let the match burn right to the end. Each time it meant one less cigarette in the packet. But all the same you cannot do without everything. You cannot really, every time you want a smoke, tell yourself you shouldn't. He looked towards the window. Perhaps it was not raining any longer. In any case nothing could be seen because of the steam on the window-panes. Was it credible? He was living the life of a humble pensioner who bought his own lunch, cooked it, did his own washing, sewed on his own buttons. A humble pensioner! Not even that. He no longer had any pension. Who would give him one? He had never been in the civil service. He had never been anywhere. Neither was he a man of independent means. He had no income. But people thought he had a small private income. That was something to be angry about. To give the appearance of something and yet to have none of its advantages. Sixteen hundred francs a year! The rent was only sixteen hundred francs and he could not even pay it. There was the same trouble every quarter. He settled his neck against the back of the armchair. His eyes rested on the cornice of the sideboard. He was looking elsewhere. Men of worth, intelligent men, who above all had strength of mind, were all equally successful. If only he had followed the path which had opened before him in his youth, if he had been patient, if every year he had been content to be a little richer, a little more respected than the year before, today he would be as happy as the professor. He would be living in a beautiful flat. He would have servants. He would have a fashionable wife who would talk about him in society, and so on. The trouble was that he had thought all that ridiculous. So he had no right to complain. And if today, instead of being a person as important as the professor, he had to borrow a few hundred francs from that same professor every month (and each time he was afraid it might be too early, that he might be tiring him or taking advantage of him), that was quite natural. And if it happened that today it was the professor's son-in-law who received him, and that he had to ask for the few hundred francs he needed from the second husband of the woman who had been his, Lesca's, wife, that too, extraordinary as it seemed, was likewise quite natural. Even more extraordinary things could be encountered in life.

Maurice Lesca straightened up.

'Emily,' he said.

Still she did not reply. Would she have replied if his situation had been different? He had to be fair. Perhaps she would not have answered even then. No, he could not complain. What was more fitting than that a man who was searching for esteem, whose bearing, voice and gestures had been moulded by that ambition, should be compelled to take such humiliating steps! He was made for giving advice and protection and yet he had to go and ask people for help. There was no way of avoiding it. He had to live. Some people were really sorry they could not give him more. But not everyone was like that. He had to put up with everything. He had to sit down, wait, listen to advice, listen when he would so much have liked to give it himself. He had to be pleasant, to struggle against his desire to say: 'Give me something if you want, don't give anything if you don't want to.'

'Emily!' he called.

She gave no sign of life. He stood up abruptly. A man is never lost for, however old he may be, however impaired his health, he still may have many years to live, and while there is life there is hope. He went into the kitchen. He took off his jacket and hung it on the doorknob. He began to wash. The water splashed up from the sink. 'That's what is so unpleasant about washing in a kitchen.' He had long ago given up worrying about being clean. He had grown accustomed to his clothes, even his underwear, which had to smell so much that others beside himself noticed it before he could bring himself to change it. It was an event and, during the few seconds when the upper part of his body was naked, he thought he would die of cold. He changed that day. When he came out of the kitchen he had shaved and was wearing a clean collar. He looked at the time. It was a quarter to twelve.

'Emily!'

As there was no reply, he went back into the kitchen and cooked two eggs. When they were ready, he took them into his room. Only by an effort of the imagination did his lunch separate the morning and the afternoon, for it only lasted for five or ten minutes. Then he sat in the armchair. He looked at the rain running down the window-panes. He had tied the curtains back to the hasp to let in a little more light. He gazed straight ahead. 'And to think that every day is alike, and I am here, and perhaps it is too late, and perhaps I shall always be here.'

Suddenly Emily appeared. She was wearing a dress which she had cut out of a colourless old cloak. She had taken a great deal of trouble to sew a row of little tassels on to the wrists and also made braided buttonholes. The neckline came to a sharp point right down between her breasts, an odd style for an elderly woman. It was held together by a rosette of blackened silver scattered with coloured stones. Her hair, grey like damp cotton, was knotted at the back of her head with a scrap of ribbon. Below the knot it fell in a tress which she kept fingering and twisting into curls. Her face had been wrinkled

9

for many years and the wrinkles had lengthened and deepened, making her look rather masculine. She had short-sighted pale blue eyes. She gave the impression of someone who very much wanted to play the lady, and even when she was occupied with daily tasks, never to be anything but a woman momentarily obliged to work. She wore a broad wedding ring and the gold, amidst such poverty, seemed worthless. She looked at her brother over her pince-nez. Her arms hung down at her sides, not awkwardly, but not gracefully either, like the arms of a woman who has watched other women and wishes to be like them. Lesca had lowered his eyes. He was watching his sister furtively.

'Didn't you hear me just now?' he asked, no longer making a secret of watching her on the sly.

'Should I have answered you?'

'Oh! There was no need,' said Lesca smiling. 'There was no need. It wasn't necessary. But it would have pleased me.'

She shrugged her shoulders. Then she went into the kitchen. Lesca followed her.

'How are you this morning?' he asked.

She turned abruptly.

'Very well,' she said aggressively.

'I'm very glad.'

She opened the little white-wood dresser, looked at the few utensils inside it, but did not pick one up. 'I can't remember what I wanted,' she said.

'I'm very glad,' repeated Lesca. 'I'm very glad to hear that you are well. I was afraid . . .'

'That's enough, Maurice,' she said, making an impatient movement.

'I was afraid you were unwell. You didn't reply.'

'What does that mean: I was afraid, I was afraid . . . You weren't afraid of anything at all. Please, leave me in peace.'

Lesca appeared extremely surprised.

'What's the matter with you?'

She did not answer. 'It was the matches I was looking for,' she said. She lit the gas. Her brother was standing next to her. She seemed to have forgotten him.

'So you think your health . . .' he said, not finishing his sentence.

She did not reply.

'It's just that I have something very important to tell you,' he went on.

'Ah!' she said.

He lowered his eyes and, as he had done before, looked furtively at his sister.

'I shall have some money soon,' he said, as if this was without importance.

Emily's eyes did not leave the saucepan of milk she had put on the gas.

'Are you listening?' he asked.

'Yes, yes.'

'Aren't you surprised?'

'Why should I be surprised?'

'Oh! Emily,' he cried, 'how good you are!'

She turned her head towards her brother for a second.

'Please, Maurice.'

'I'm going to be rich, Emily,' Lesca went on. 'I can't tell you exactly when, but in a month or two at most. Rich! I may be exaggerating a bit.'

'I'm sure you are!' exclaimed Emily.

'We must talk, mustn't we?'

Emily bent down from time to time to see if the gas was still burning.

'Yes, you are good, Emily. You hate it when I pay you compliments. But I'm telling you. I must tell you. People have always reproached me for lack of resources, haven't they? Why don't you answer?'

'What do you want me to say?'

She began to laugh.

'I can't be trusted, can I? I'm a man whose word does not count.'

He went up to his sister.

'Today I have a tremendous piece of news to tell you. I'm going to have some money soon and my life, you hear me, my life will change.'

He broke off. Emily did not seem to be listening.

'Emily,' he said, 'can't you pay attention to what I'm saying?'

'Yes, yes.'

11

'Well then, don't you take me seriously?'

'Oh, yes.'

Lesca held out both his hands theatrically.

'Thank you, thank you,' he said in a deep voice.

'It seems to me that's quite enough for today,' said Emily.

'Do you believe me? Tell me that you believe me,' begged Lesca humbly.

'You don't care whether I believe you or not,' she said crossly.

'Don't I?'

She turned off the gas and looked for a bowl in the dresser.

'You're right,' he said, returning to normal. 'But we must liven up the conversation.'

Emily's expression hardened.

'Why do you think anyone should take any notice of you?' she said.

Lesca resumed his humble tone.

'If you only knew the good you have just done me!'

'That's enough!'

'Let me say it again. If you only knew how much I suffer sometimes when nobody takes me seriously, when I am considered a trickster, a liar.'

'More play-acting!'

'True, true. It is play-acting. You are right.'

Suddenly he fell silently. Then he smiled. He was very calm now.

'After all,' he said, 'whether people take me seriously or not is all the same to me.'

Emily picked up her milk and passed in front of her brother without looking at him. He followed her.

'You see, you see! You always misunderstand what I'm saying,' he went on.

'But it's all the same to you!'

'But no, Emily, it isn't all the same to me. So you don't understand?'

He went and sat down opposite his sister.

'Forgive me, Emily. I don't appreciate your kindness enough. After all, you are the only person who does not bear me a grudge.'

'I've no reason to bear you a grudge.'

Lesca raised a hand.

'Believe me, I shan't forget it. The day is coming when I shall have some money. Don't forget what I'm going to tell you. At that moment I shall remember . . .

'Oh! that's another story.'

'Let me finish. I shall remember that our life . . .'

'Our life!' exclaimed Emily ironically.

Lesca seemed very surprised.

'Does that shock you?'

'Oh, no, nothing shocks me.'

Emily stood up abruptly and went back to the kitchen.

'Emily!' cried Lesca.

She did not reply.

'Don't you want to listen to me?'

'No.'

For a moment he was taken aback.

'What a tragedy!' he murmured.

At that moment she came back. She had not been running away from him.

'So what I'm saying doesn't interest you?' he asked.

'Not in the very least.'

He kept quiet for a second. Then he stood up and walked across the room for a moment or two. Finally he sat down in the armchair.

'You're right, Emily. It isn't very interesting.'

Once again he rested his head against the back of the chair. He closed his eyes. It had begun to rain extremely hard. He could hear it beating against the window-panes. He could also hear his sister coming and going, but he was not thinking about her any longer. He opened his eyes. She was passing right in front of him on her way back to her own room. He did not even see her. He thought: 'I am a prisoner. All my life I have been a prisoner. I thought I was free, but I was a prisoner. Someone or something has always prevented me from doing what I wanted. I wish I had a bomb. There are times when I should like to blow everything up. But, in order to blow everything up, one needs to be able to. And even that is not possible. I can't do anything, anything, anything. My hands are tied. I am powerless.'

As he had been sleeping badly for several months, Lesca had taken to lying down in the early afternoon. He stretched out on his bed and covered his legs with his overcoat. But though he might shut his eyes, he did not doze off. He thought about the small happenings of the preceding weeks, but he was in such a wretched state of mind that he saw them all as hurtful. He had been improvident. People had had a good laugh. He had behaved childishly, even grotesquely.

At four o'clock he got up and went to the window to look at the weather. It was not raining any longer. There was water running everywhere, but it was not raining. He went and washed his face in the kitchen. He brushed his overcoat. Then he went out. The owner of the little café was standing on his doorstep. Lesca forgot to greet him. A little further on he realized what he had done. He came hurriedly back, excusing himself at length and giving all sorts of reasons for his forgetfulness. He moved off. 'Shall I go back again or shall I not go back?' he wondered. He went along the rue de Rivoli. There were so many people that from time to time he had to step off the pavement in spite of the cars. Now and again, when he saw someone he liked the look of in the crowd, he would stare at him equivocally. He was old, ill and poor (at least he thought so), he could do nothing for anyone, but he was anxious that this look should show that he was capable of fellow-feeling. Besides, what could anyone expect of him? But he belonged to those faithful souls, lost in the crowd, who are needed by those who want to do something significant and whom he could appreciate. He crossed the Seine. This late afternoon was very remarkable. There was water everywhere and yet in the blue sky there was spring. The sun had already set. It had not wanted to show itself. But in its generosity it left the doors of its dwelling open to all. Lesca reached the place Saint-Michel. 'If it was only that I am old, ill and poor!' he thought. 'But there are times when I lose hope.' He was no longer looking for a sympathetic face. He thought the first comer worthy of communication by a look. A warm breeze, which was not a warning of rain as that was over, passed over the water-blackened street. Lesca felt an immense need for change growing within him. He turned into the rue des Ecoles. In the distance the light was growing

14

dim. He thought: 'Just suppose someone's curiosity should be aroused by my appearance and that he followed me, he would wonder: where is that man going?' He turned round. Nobody seemed to be following him. He smiled and murmured: 'That man! That man!' It always made him prick up his ears to be called a man. And when he called himself a man, he felt rather as if he had been boasting. He thought: 'That man looks very tired. He's obviously swamped by life's wretched cares. It's lucky he's not alone! You only have to look around. There are thousands like him. They are all taking thought for the things of the morrow.' He turned round again. He could see himself in all the plate glass, shop windows and café partitions. He had just left his flat after a long day in which he had done nothing. He could see himself with his worn clothes and that air of being a man who affords no interest to anyone, but who is nevertheless part of society. 'I'll go and talk to Madame Maze. I do have one thing, after all, that's experience. I have experience, fine, wide experience, if nothing else. Of course, Madame Maze may think me tactless. She may even wonder if I have some ulterior motive. But I must do my duty.'

When he reached the end of the long rue des Ecoles, another street, just as long, opened up on his right. The far end of this street was even darker than the rue des Ecoles. It sloped gently upwards. Lesca stopped to light a cigarette, then he went on his way, but much more slowly. It would soon be night. The sky might still be blue but the streets themselves were plunged in the chiaroscuro of a blind alley. A few moments later, Lesca crossed the road and then stood motionless opposite a small bookshop on the pavement he had just left. For two or three minutes he never took his eyes off the shop, although he seemed to be waiting for somebody and kept on turning his head. At last he crossed back. Steam dimmed the glass of the shop door and the light from the back of the shop seemed to come from a long way off, making it sparkle like frost. For a little while he again pretended to be waiting for someone, then he approached the bookshop and even put his hand on the door-handle. But he dared not do more. It was only after several minutes that he made up his mind to go in.

Shortly before the war, while he was out for a walk, Lesca had gone into this small shop which sold books, ink, exercise books and a whole range of leather articles produced by the same firm. He wanted to buy a packet of writing paper. As he was leaving he had looked up. In doing so he had met the gaze of the woman who kept the shop. All of a sudden he had had the feeling that he was no longer alone. However, he had left as if nothing had happened. He went on his way, reflecting. 'I understand now why I have come to grief in everything I have undertaken. I understand why I am poor, why I have no friends, no wife, no children. What has just happened to me is what has happened a hundred times already. I am only attractive to people who are in pain, to people whom life has already written off, where nothing pleasant can happen to me. That shopkeeper is a poor woman on her own, who was once in comfortable circumstances, but is so no longer, who has had disappointments of every kind, financial and emotional, and who has taken to running a bookshop to earn her living because the customers seem to be more select. It only needed a glance for her to recognize me as one of her sort: a well-educated man who has also had disappointments and who has passed the age for anger and lies.'

A few days later, Lesca made his way towards the book-shop. He felt no great desire to see the woman again. But one never knew. Several times along the way he had almost turned back. There was something humiliating about it. He felt sure he would not find what he was looking for and that he would not want what he did find. But he told himself, by way of encouragement, that however insignificant it might be, it would nevertheless be more than he had. At the last moment he was filled with apprehension. He was so well aware of the kind of friendship which could arise between a woman like this shopkeeper and himself. He knew so well that everything was very far from what he really hoped for. But when he had turned back and saw the emptiness of his life opening before him, he thought that after all he might as well try. He retraced his steps and went into the shop. That was how the connection began which, in time, was to grow into a deep and true friendship. Madame Maze was not the woman he had imagined. Although she had had her troubles, she did not talk about them. She did not think of herself as a victim of men or of life. She behaved quite naturally whatever was happening. So when, a few weeks later, she told Lesca that she had never met a man with such a generous mind and warm feelings as himself, he took the compliment at its face value. He understood that how she was situated financially really did not matter very much and that it was quite possible to be fond of people from whom no material advantage could be expected. Of course he was sorry that a woman like that had not been rich. He would have loved her with all his remaining strength. But he comforted himself with the reflection that, if she had been rich, she would perhaps not have kept all the qualities which pleased him so much. His initial fear of burdening himself, as so often before, with people from whom he had nothing to hope for, faded away. Nevertheless he occasionally said to himself: 'It's still the same story. It just looks different, that's all.' Eventually the fear disappeared altogether. The adventure had lost its novelty. It was already too old for him to go on asking himself questions about it. He had a friend with whom he could be quite open. He spent many pleasant hours with her. Their friendship was genuine. Moreover each of them was very careful not to put it to the test. And when this prudence became too obvious, Madame Maze was just as ready to laugh about it as Lesca, and so they both had the illusion that they would be able to abandon it if ever it became necessary.

'You're late today, Monsieur Lesca,' said a woman's voice from a room hidden by a display of books. 'The tea has been ready for a long time. Hurry up.'

'Greetings, dear friend,' said Lesca, saluting jokingly.

'Come on, come on, Monsieur Lesca.'

He joined her. Tea was ready. Nothing was missing. Everything was in perfect order. A tiny embroidered napkin had been put on a plate. Every day he refused to make use of it. Madame Maze was wearing a black silk frock. She had put on a little make-up. Not a strand had escaped from the grey mass of her hair in which, here and there, a fine pin could be seen, intended to keep it in position. The wrinkles spreading from the corners of her eyes, like rays, gave her a look both faded and childish.

'I'm sorry,' said Lesca, 'but work, you know.'

'Come now, don't talk about your work!'

Lesca smiled.

'Sit down,' said Madame Maze, changing a cup at the last minute.

Although the smile remained on his face, Lesca was actually not smiling any more. He was watching Madame Maze, with his eyes half closed. From time to time, by tightening the corners of his mouth a little, he revived his smile.

After tea he said casually:

'I've been thinking, dear friend, I've been thinking. Our conversation yesterday was very interesting, wasn't it? I am a bit like you.'

Madame Maze bowed her head.

'Please don't let's talk about that any more!' she said in the tone of one who wanted to seem genuinely embarrassed by a compliment.

'At the time, I did not fully appreciate . . .'

'You would have done the same in my place.'

'I'm not so sure,' said Lesca, showing by his wry expression, as he often did, that he had no very high opinion of his own virtues.

He lit a cigarette. He was no longer smiling. He had the look of those people who suffer pain from something they cannot talk about and who hide it by pretending to be like everybody else.

'What you did is very fine, Gabrielle.'

'I assure you that I was not thinking about how fine it was,' she replied with the air of those who want to seem to do the right thing quite naturally, without even being aware of what they are doing.

'My wife would certainly not have acted as you did. I have never talked about her, you must admit. I don't like talking about my life. You don't either. People get bored. They wait for you to have done with it. And yet there are some half-wits who go on talking. Though let me tell you that my wife, in spite of all her pretentions to a good education, did not spare me when we had to put our affairs in order. I had all the lawyers in Paris on my back overnight.'

'And you would like me to be like her?'

Lesca gazed earnestly at Madame Maze. He remained silent for some moments, then exclaimed:

'I? Look here, Gabrielle. You know me well enough. You know that I think you are absolutely right. It's not a matter of being like my wife, or like anyone else. It's simply a matter of not being stupid.'

Hardly had he spoken this last word, when he sprang to his feet. He shook his clenched fists.

'Oh! Just listen to me beginning to talk like those people we don't care for.'

'That's what I was thinking, though I dared not say so.'

'Forgive me. That's just the sort of thing my aunt would say.'

He sat down again. He asked for another cup of tea. As it was his fourth, he refused sugar and milk.

'You are absurd,' said Madame Maze.

For all she might insist, he did not give way. He lit another cigarette.

'But really,' he said, 'when I think about it, it seems to me that I'm not so very wrong.'

'You amuse me when you talk like that, Maurice. It really doesn't suit you.'

He appeared surprised.

'I should never have believed,' Madame Maze went on, 'that you, who are so whimsical, so open-hearted, so crazy, would ever become so very rational.'

He lowered his eyes. He raised them again at once so that Madame Maze should not see that he was avoiding her gaze, but in spite of all his efforts he had to lower them again. He held out his hands to Madame Maze under the table.

'I know very well that you are right, Gabrielle,' he said sorrowfully. 'I know, I know. But I'm thinking about you. When I see you here, you, in this shop, it troubles me. It's not the right place for you. Of course, it would be better to keep quiet, I'm well aware of that. It is a fine gesture.'

He paused, then said with a smile that was both ironical and troubled:

'But gestures, I ask you!'

He broke off again.

'You see, between you and me,' he went on, 'gestures, the very noblest gestures, what are they?'

'You disappoint me,' said Madame Maze lightly.

'I know I do,' he said. 'Don't think that I'm not a disappointment to myself !'

He stood up. For a second he pretended to be dazzled. Then he bowed ceremoniously to Madame Maze.

'You see before you a man who is fond of giving advice, of guiding the people he loves through the traps which life lays for them. You see before you a man to whose words you should attach no importance, because he talks for talking's sake. He's fond of hearing himself too. He is a man who, in fact, is not serious.'

When he left Madam Maze, Lesca felt uneasy. He had shown himself in a bad light. He had been lacking in courage and decisiveness. He had spoken as people had so often spoken to him and Madame Maze had answered in the same way he had always answered himself. She was not one of those women who go back on the opinions they have formed. Nevertheless a doubt managed to insinuate itself into his mind. He ought to have made fun of himself with more spirit. At the end he had struck a false note. 'Tomorrow I shall have to clear things up,' he thought. 'She was laughing when I left. Of course she was laughing. But now? Perhaps she is wondering what I am interfering in. I could not even make her understand that it was only a matter of her own good. Perhaps she will be wondering if she really knows me. Why, all of a sudden, is he taking an interest in this story? How clumsy I am! All the same I can't keep on and on saying that I'm acting out of goodness, generosity and affection for her. Nevertheless I shall have to say it.' For a moment he almost went back, it was so painful to him to allow twenty-four hours to elapse over this misunderstanding. But it was very difficult. She might well have been disagreeably surprised to see him again.

The next day, as soon as he was with Madame Maze, he said to her:

'I am particularly pleased to see you today, dear friend. When I left you, I had the impression that you might interpret what I had said to you in various ways.'

When he arrived, Lesca had not stood to attention. He had not wanted to accept a cup of tea.

'Today I am going to tell you exactly what I think.'

One of his hands was lying motionless on the table. He was obviously trying hard to avoid any movement which might distract Madame Maze.

'No doubt you think I attach importance to your going to see him?'

Instead of replying, Madame Maze inclined her head and clasped her hands.

'How serious you seem today!' she said.

'We don't take money very seriously,' Lesca continued. 'Our lives prove it. Otherwise we should not be here, either of us, in the back of this shop. Well, I really do think you should go and see him, simply in your own interest, you understand. It's precisely because money doesn't mean anything to me that I can give you this advice. If someone else were to give you the same advice I should find it abominable. But with me it isn't the same thing. You understand why, Gabrielle! You know me. You know who I am. You understand what I mean. It's not the same thing.'

'I have never seen you in this state before, Maurice.'

He cast a strange look at Madame Maze. It was the look of a man who hears a noise when he believes himself to be alone.

'Let me finish,' he went on. 'I tell you that with me it's not the same thing. Do you know why? Because I personally don't care about it. I'm doing it simply for you. I'm only thinking of you. Money is something which doesn't exist for me. So I really can tell you to go and see him.'

Madame Maze realized that Lesca was not joking.

'You surely don't wish me to give him that satisfaction after what has happened!'

It was the first time since the beginning of the exchange that she had answered Lesca otherwise than tongue-in-cheek. He seemed put out. He uttered a few disconnected words and then kept quiet for a little while.

'Oh! No, I wouldn't wish it,' he said softly.

His excitement had vanished. He seemed to have recovered his composure. He smiled. Madame Maze looked at him with astonishment. Then she smiled too.

'So you were trying to make me frantic?' she asked.

'I?' cried Lesca.

21

'Look at you putting on your high and mighty ways again! You must realize that it's very difficult to understand you.'

'Oh, no! Nothing is easier. I'm sorry, it isn't my fault. You are right. I acknowledge it, you are right. I am suddenly aware of it. I'm always imagining that people are like us, that they think like us. I'm mistaken, that's all there is to it. I can never get it into my head that we are dealing with mediocrities. "Ah! She has no more money. Ah! She needs me. That's what it is to run away! It's a good thing I was there to look after her money. She is very pleased to see me again today." You are right, Gabrielle. I acknowledge it. I'm sorry. I'm a fool. These ideas don't even enter my head. I don't imagine their entering other people's heads. I saw you looking for what belongs to you like your going to the bank. If only everything were so simple.'

In the evening, when he got home, Lesca dropped into the leather armchair. He had not paused on the landings on his way upstairs and his heart was pounding violently. He threw his hat on to the table, but his aim was so bad that it fell on the floor. Emily was presumably in the other room. She was obsessive about staying quietly in her room and giving no sign of her presence before she was called.

'Emily,' cried Lesca, when he had recovered his breath.

'Are you calling me?' she asked without stirring, like someone completely independent who has no intention of being disturbed.

'Would you be kind enough to get me a glass of water? I don't feel very well.'

She did not answer. A few moments passed during which he listened for the smallest noise. He dared not call her again for fear she would still not reply. At last he heard a movement. He lowered his eyelids, half-opened his mouth and bent slightly forward. Just at that moment Emily appeared. She looked at her brother with the air of somebody who is used to being sent hither and thither in response to desperate appeals and who is well aware that nothing is ever wrong.

'I'll bring it for you,' she said.

She passed by the hat but did not pick it up.

'I don't think I have got much longer,' said Lesca when she came back. 'You will suppose that I'm asleep but I shall be dead. God will have called me to him. You will be free. There will be nobody to ask you for a glass of water any more. Emily! Emily! Will that make you sad?'

She handed him the glass. She had left it under the tap for too long and water was trickling down the outside. At the same time she glanced at her brother indifferently. It was obvious that she had made up her mind never to answer him. Then, without saying a word, she went back into her room.

Lesca drank the glass of water in one gulp, then put it on the floor. He lit a cigarette. When he had smoked half of it, he said aloud, as if no one could hear him: 'There! It's done! I've had the care I needed! I only had to open my mouth and someone came running. All I have to do is rest and keep quiet! It's very pleasant not to be on one's own when one begins to get old! Somebody else might have had to call for his neighbours, for strangers!' Suddenly he began to cry out: 'Why? Why? Is it a punishment? Is it the punishment? But I haven't done anything wrong. I have been improvident, it's true. I have always given to everybody. I have never thought of myself. I have always been too kind. That's the reason. Emily! Emily!'

He fell silent, waiting for a reply. His ears were humming. He was afraid he could not hear. He held his head forward. There was no sound except the pounding in his ears. He called again. This time he heard:

'What's the matter with you today?'

'The matter with me today? Nothing, nothing. I simply think I have been too kind. Yes, I have been too kind. I may seem to be joking. Nevertheless it's true. Every time I have met someone unfortunate on my path, I have helped him. Yes, indeed. I have given money to everyone. Of course I could have done with more. What I earned was not enough. But I stinted myself. It's true, isn't it, Emily?'

'How should I know? I don't know about your life.'

Lesca threw away his cigarette. These last words seemed to have surprised him. He looked anxiously at the door. He tried to find some sort of answer.

'You don't know about my life, you, my sister!'

There was no reply. He lit another cigarette and for a few minutes remained motionless with his eyes half closed.

'You don't know about my life!' he repeated. 'That's right, I had never thought about it, I am a stranger to you. We don't know each other. Chance brought us together again here. That's all.'

He stood up abruptly and went into Emily's room. She was stretched out on her divan. She had wrapped her legs in her overcoat. A bedside lamp lit up the book she was reading.

'Come on, Emily, you can see very well that I am speaking to you seriously.'

She moved the lamp slightly in order to see her brother.

'Listen, Maurice,' she said, 'you're getting tiresome.'

'So you don't want to admit that I have been too generous, that the state I am in today has come about because I have been too generous?'

'I don't know anything about it, my poor Maurice.'

'I implore you, Emily, answer me.'

She removed the coat which was covering her legs and sat on the edge of the divan.

'Please,' she said, feigning exhaustion, 'no fine words. Don't keep on asking me.'

'Then answer me,' he said.

'Answer what?'

'Come now, Emily!'

'What do you want me to answer? If you have been unfortunate, it's not my fault. What am I to do about it? What's going on today? You have never been like this before.'

Lesca suddenly recovered his temper.

'You know very well what I mean, Emily. This isn't kind. You are pretending not to understand. It's not kind. I have always been good to you.'

She hid her face in her hands.

'Oh, as for that!' she cried.

'What's the matter?' asked Lesca.

'Nothing,' she said, recovering her composure at once. 'I swear to you, Maurice,' she went on, 'I understand absolutely nothing of what you are telling me.'

'Very well,' he said.

He withdrew.

'Do you want to have dinner before me?'

'No, you eat first.'

He took off his overcoat and picked up his hat. Then he went into the kitchen. He put a saucepan of water on the heat, then stood still, his eyes fixed on the scraps of food lying between the plates of the gas-stove and on top of the reflectors placed on the flames.

'And if I had any money on me, in my pockets,' he said, going back to his sister and striking his chest with both hands.

She looked at him as people look at a man who has suddenly lost control of what he is saying.

'Yes, if I had any money!' he went on.

'I still don't understand.'

'I haven't any. I think it important to tell you that immediately so that you don't have any false hopes.'

'How stupid you are!'

He went up to the divan and took hold of Emily's arm. She did not attempt to free herself but her expression made it quite clear that the arm no longer belonged to her.

'I am your brother, Emily.'

She looked at him contemptuously.

'Have your dinner . . .'

'Enough,' she said, abruptly pulling her arm away. 'Enough of your fancy talk.'

He seemed to be thinking.

'My fancy talk. It's true. It's actually true. Isn't it extraordinary? Fancy talk from me!'

'I think I might say so,' replied Emily, whose face had suddenly softened.

He went away again. The water was boiling. He took it off and did not know what else to do in the kitchen. He went into his room, picked up a plate and went back into the kitchen. He liked eating standing up at the sideboard, which was as tall as a writing-desk. When he had finished, he began to walk up and down. From time to time he heard Emily turning a page of a book. Every time he passed the door he could see her reclining on the divan like a young woman. He was in fact surprised that she had adopted such a graceful position. He occasionally had the feeling that she was a stranger. It seemed odd that she should be there, making herself at home so freely, without for a second thinking of concealing herself from him.

Eventually he went into her room once again and asked very tenderly:

'I'm not disturbing you, am I?'

She threw him the same glance as ever over the top of her spectacles, but did not utter a word. He picked up a chair, carried it over to the divan and sat down.

'Emily, don't you think some situations are extraordinary? I'm thinking of ours, for example.'

She did not even raise her eyes.

'For years,' he went on, 'for years, and years, and years, and years, and years, how many years, Emily?'

'How many years? Why?' she asked, without ceasing to read.

'Thirty-five, thirty-seven,' he said.

'Perhaps,' she murmured.

'Isn't it strange that we are here today?'

She did not answer.

'Emily!'

As she went on reading, he cried:

'Emily!'

She still did not lift her eyes.

'What's the matter with me? Look, look,' he cried more loudly than ever. 'What's the matter with me? What's the matter with me?'

He was trembling or rather shaking. His jaws were so tightly clenched that his neck had thickened and the tendons stood out clearly.

Emily went on reading. Soon Lesca calmed down. He was still breathing noisily but seemed not to be in pain any more. He stood up and put the chair back in its place. Before he went out, he looked at Emily. She was not reading any longer. She was leaning back on a skimpy cushion and was gazing straight ahead of her.

'Aren't you having any dinner, Emily?'

She stood up and put out the little bedside lamp. As she passed by her brother, she stopped.

'You ought to go to bed,' she said.

Lesca had gone out early. He had washed before going out, something he rarely did. He put his shopping on the table.

Emily was still in bed. She got her coffee ready the day before. She poured it into a Thermos flask which she put within reach. So she had no need to get up for her breakfast. Then, covering her shoulders with a shawl, she knitted until eleven o'clock, or midday sometimes, looking at her work absent-mindedly, deep in endless reflections on often insignificant subjects. Lesca did not say a word to her. He went out again immediately. An hour later he was standing in a crowded street, in front of a neglected house, apparently deserted, at the door of which were about ten tradesman's plates. He climbed a wide staircase which was all the gloomier because the sky was overcast. The numerous shallow steps were grimy with wet footmarks. On the third floor, he opened a door, going in without knocking, as an enamelled notice urged him. A girl came forward to meet him from the end of a corridor lit by electricity.

'Is your father here, Mademoiselle Suzanne?'

She looked at the visitor with astonishment. She looked as if she had never seen him before.

'Yes, he's here.'

At that moment a short fat woman, whose bosom was held in place by the tight waistband of a black apron, opened a door.

'You want to see Monsieur Olivetti?' she said, taking the girl's place.

'How are you, Madame Olivetti?'

She came nearer, surprised, then cried suddenly:

'Oh! Monsieur Lesca! It's you, Monsieur Lesca! How pleased my husband will be to see you! Come in, come in.'

She showed him into a fiting-room.

'Sit down, Monsieur Lesca. My husband will be here at once. How amazed he will be! What a surprise you have given us!'

Lesca found the tailor's room familiar. The same disorder, the same fashion plates on the walls, the same triple-faced mirror, the same stock, the same smell of cooking, the pieces of cloth lying everywhere. He went to the window and looked into the street from which the cries of the barrow-boys were rising. In fact, he could hear nothing. In the hollow under his left eye a curious pulse was lifting the skin, as if, following a muscular spasm, an artery had been discovered. He had put

27

down his coat collar. He held his hat in his hand. He had been wearing it for two hours at the most and his forehead was marked as if it had been subjected to long and painful pressure. Suddenly a man in shirt-sleeves appeared in the doorway. He had not shaved. He looked at once neglected and clean, as men do who have left the business of looking after their appearance to their wives.

'Monsieur Lesca,' he cried, his eyes shining with immense joy, 'how kind of you to have come to see us.'

'I have been wanting to come for a long time,' said Lesca.

'Oh, how kind of you,' repeated Monsieur Olivetti, his face full of gratitude.

One could tell that he was a man quite without malice, whom everybody liked, who was filled with happiness by an ordinary visit like this one.

'I haven't seen you for a good ten years,' he said.

'Even more,' said Lesca. 'I have often thought about you. Each time I said to myself: I must go and see good Monsieur Olivetti, but the opportunity did not arise.'

'We have not forgotten you, Monsieur Lesca! Oh, no! We have been talking about you all the time. We were wondering if you would come back one day.'

'You see, I have come back.'

'We saw your brother-in-law not long ago.'

Lesca did not reply. He had made a space for himself among the remnants of cloth which littered the sofa. Monsieur Olivetti was standing in front of him. His manifestations of joy were becoming rarer, but he was clearly deeply moved.

'You haven't changed, Monsieur Olivetti.'

'Don't say that, Monsieur Lesca. I have changed in here,' he said indicating his chest. 'I'm some years older.'

'So am I,' said Lesca.

'Oh, no! It's not the same.'

Madame Olivetti, who had not wanted to hinder the first emotional outburst, had come back. She stood slightly apart, not daring to speak, with a tender expression.

'I'm going to leave you now,' said Lesca, suddenly weary. 'I wanted to see you. I have seen you.'

The throbbing beneath his eye, which had disappeared, returned abruptly. Lesca stood up and picked up his hat. He had a red patch on each of his cheeks. Monsieur Olivetti called his daughter. He wanted to show what the child of former days had become. But Lesca did not try to think of something pleasant to say to her. He was already thinking of other things. When he was in the street, instead of catching the bus which would have taken him directly home, he was filled with a desire to wander about. He compared a few prices with those of his own district. 'That was all it needed!' he said suddenly. He would have liked to have been able to walk about in the crowd with his eyes closed so that he should no longer see the labels which were drawing his gaze.

As soon as he found himself in Madame Maze's back shop, Lesca would become another man. He forgot his lodgings and his sister. He had chosen to be free. He gestured as he spoke. Nevertheless it sometimes happened that, while Madame Maze was speaking and he felt bound to listen to her, he resumed his usual look. Then she would ask: 'What's the matter with you all of sudden?' He jumped. 'Nothing, nothing's the matter,' he said. He took the opportunity this incident offered and, to bear out his words, little by little he recovered his cheerfulness.

'In fact,' he said to Madame Maze, 'you have never told me what sort of man your husband is. I must admit I cannot picture him at all.'

In uttering these words, Lesca had adopted a detached tone, gently mocking. However, at the same time, his eye had begun to tremble as it had at Monsieur Olivetti's.

'I should never have thought that would have been of any interest to you, Maurice.'

Lesca reddened slightly.

'It interests me a great deal. I'll tell you why in a moment.'

'So you are anxious for me to give you a description of my husband? Nothing is easier. He is a real gentleman.'

'Oh!' said Lesca ironically.

'You want to know what my husband is like. I am telling you. Though I may not love him any more, I am obliged to acknowledge his good qualities.'

29

'I'm not reproaching you with anything,' said Lesca. 'I don't expect you would have married some half-wit. So, is he kind, intelligent, does he understand life?'

'I was twenty when I got to know him,' continued Madame Maze. 'I was just a girl. We were in love.'

'Yes, yes, I understand,' said Lesca. 'But you are not answering. Is he intelligent? I'm asking you this question because I have an idea at the back of my mind. I'm thinking of going to find your husband.'

'You want to go and see him?' cried Madame Maze in utter astonishment.

Lesca began to laugh.

'It's stupid, isn't it?'

Madame Maze did not answer. She was looking at Lesca. She was wondering if he was in earnest. She found him strangely calm.

'I know quite well it's stupid.'

In fact Lesca was extremely agitated. He could hear his heart in his chest, as if it were filling it completely.

'But it's necessary,' he went on. 'Don't you think so? If I don't do it, who will?'

'Nobody!' cried Madame Maze.

'Why nobody? I assure you that someone has to do it. I can't bear to see you staying in this wretched shop any longer, working, while what belongs to you remains with a man who doesn't need it and only wants to give it back to you. It's a ridiculous situation. I know all about your pride. But pride is irrelevant in an affair of this kind. It's true that I myself, in your place, should not ask for anything. But I'm not in your place. I can make things happen that are impossible for you to effect. Believe me! Today I am only too well acquainted with the value of money. Perhaps I am not really the man you thought I was, perhaps not even the man I thought I was myself. I am perhaps more attached than I thought to material things. The strange thing is, Gabrielle, that I can no longer bear that any money, whether it belongs to me or not, should be lost.'

Lesca broke off. He smiled. He could still hear his heart. Now, at each pulsation, he had the feeling that someone was touching him.

'I want to speak to you so reasonably,' he went on, stroking his cheek to heighten the colour he suspected must already be there, 'that I don't know what I'm saying any more. I want to bring you to accept things that I should not accept if I were in your place. But still, I feel I'm right. I may perhaps be jealous in retrospect. It must be said that your husband is getting off too easily. He marries you when you are twenty, at the height of your beauty. He makes use of you. Then he takes a mistress. You leave and he keeps what belongs to you. I find that extraordinary. A man - you understand me, Gabrielle, and I am myself a man, so I can speak with full knowledge of the facts - a man, a gentleman as you say, would not have kept what did not belong to him.'

'But he didn't keep anything,' cried Madame Maze. 'It was I who left everything. You don't know him. He didn't even think about it. He is a man who has never bothered about money. His family has reproached him with it often enough. Besides, what I left doesn't amount to much. I wasn't rich. I'm the daughter of an army officer.'

Lesca felt a cold breath on his body. He hunched up a little. He put a hand to his forehead. Now he could feel a pain between his ribs at each heartbeat. The pain was like a prick.

'Even if the amount is insignificant,' he said, trying very hard to take an interest in it, 'it belongs to you. You ought to have it back. It's only natural. I was saying to you just now that I wanted to go and see your husband . . .'

'That isn't possible!' cried Madame Maze.

Lesca's shoulders sagged. For a moment nothing could be seen of his eyes but the whites, which were all bloodshot at the edge. Then, suddenly, an extraordinary light flooded over his face.

'You didn't let me finish, my dear. I am mad. I was going to tell you that I am mad. I would never have gone to see that man, never. How could you have believed that I would go? You know me. I was talking, I was talking like a reasonable man. But I'm not reasonable. I never have been. You know that. Things have to be left as they are. We have to live. We have to love. We don't have to think about all our wretched mistakes. Do we, Gabrielle? You see, from time to time I am a sort of Don Quixote. I can't bear it when people I love are under attack. And then I am alone too much every day. My sister, my sister . . . it's nothing. So I think all the time, and I realize that I have always been mistaken, that all the good I have wanted to do has always been ridiculed and finally I have got to where I am. And with you, Gabrielle, it would be the same thing. So I rebel. And this is the result.'

When he was outside again, he almost ran as far as the first empty street. He stopped and leaned against a wall. His face was covered with sweat. It was no longer a needle prick he could feel in his heart but a tearing pain. 'What a mad idea, what a mad idea!' he kept repeating. His head was spinning. He had to put both hands against the wall in order to keep his balance. Ten minutes passed. At last he could let go of the wall. He took out his handkerchief and wiped his hands and forehead.

When he went home (much later than on other days because, after leaving Madame Maze, he had spent over two hours sitting motionless in a café, with his eyes open, though without thinking about anything), he found his sister sitting in the leather armchair. Normally she would get up immediately. She attached great importance to making clear the difference between what did and what did not belong to her. And when, taking advantage of its owner's absence, she made use of what was not her own, she made something of a show of giving it back quickly when he came home. That evening she did not stir. She had neither book nor knitting on her lap. The edging of scalloped linen which she pinned inside her neckline was grey and creased. She had not taken it off for a fortnight, neither for doing her cooking nor even for going to bed. She must have been crying. Her eyes were dry but swollen. Lesca pretended not to notice anything. He himself was in very low spirits after his visits to Madame Maze and Olivetti. His courage had failed him. 'I was ridiculous,' he had kept on saying to himself since he had left the café. The way I behave, people always wonder after I've gone: What was he really after?' He sat on a chair and untied his shoes, but he did not take them off. For some time now, his ankles had begun to swell abnormally

32

in the course of the day. He also unbuttoned his collar and loosened his tie. Then he went into the kitchen, but he was not hungry. He stayed there for a little while. From time to time he moved something or other about to create the impression that he was preparing his dinner. In the end he went and stood right in front of his sister. Her neck was resting on the back of the chair. Her hands were crossed in the hollow formed by the curve of her body. She seemed not to be aware of her brother's presence.

'What's the matter?' he asked.

As she apparently did not hear, he went into the other room in the hope that she would follow him in order not to leave him alone among her private possessions. But as she did not stir, he went back to her.

'Nothing's the matter, I hope,' he said.

At last she looked at her brother.

'You hope!' she said, unclasping her hands.

'Yes, I hope there's nothing the matter. You seem so strange.'

'You hope!' she repeated in a tone surprisingly ironic, given her gloomy face.

'Yes, I do!'

'That's kind of you. It's very kind of you to hope.'

She closed up her hands, clenching them tightly into little fists.

'You hope!' she went on. 'You are too good. Thank you very much.'

Abruptly she straightened up. It seemed as if her whole face was engaged in making sure that Lesca did not shift his gaze. The withered flesh of her neck had become taut. Its wrinkles, mottlings and puffiness were forgotten in her rising anger.

'Do you know what you are?' she said suddenly.

'What, me?' said Lesca waving his hands in agitation.

'It doesn't matter to you. That's obvious. Of course. When one has such a good opinion of oneself. Yes, that's what's so appalling about you: your opinion of yourself. Nothing else exists in the world but you, does it? Nothing, nothing. You, you, only you. The rest doesn't count.'

'Me, me?' Lesca repeated.

33

'Because of the way you make fun of people . . . You do make fun of people. They're not worth anything to you, are they? So you make fun of everyone. You have always made fun of everyone. But look at the result. You have only to look at yourself in a mirror.'

Emily looked at her brother, her pity mingled with disgust.

'So you think you're the only one who counts? And people who haven't any money are not worthy of you! They have to be rich. They have to have a good job. Do you make fun of people with good jobs too? You would rather make fun of me, which is easier, less dangerous. You don't take any risks, do you? It entertains you. It's a pleasant entertainment. When you don't know what to do, well, you make fun of people! It passes the time, and you need to make time pass since you're not so fond of working. You can carry on. It's all one to me.'

Emily was so excited that Lesca did not even try to answer her. He looked at her as sadly as a father ill-treated by his children.

'Yes, that's right, be an actor too.'

He began to laugh.

'Yes, laugh, laugh as usual. It's all one to me. I tell you again. I may have acted like an idiot at times, but I have nothing to reproach myself with. What I have done is ridiculous! To you, of course it's ridiculous. But I would do it again, if necessary, in spite of your mocking. I am not like you. I am proud of what I am. You, I know, would never behave like that. Oh, no! I'm going to tell you something which will make you smile. You have to have loved to understand me. And you have never loved. You love only yourself. But now you are getting your punishment. Remember what I am saying. You will end your days all alone, in that bed. Nobody will even bring you a glass of water. At that moment, perhaps you will think of me. Above all, don't be sorry about anything.'

All night long, Lesca thought about Madame Maze. He was becoming aware of an unpleasant feeling. It was as if important events were taking place without his knowledge, as if people were making use of his advice without telling him. For several years now this fear had been tormenting him. He used to imagine that, having apparently attached no importance to what he had been saying, people were nevertheless following his advice. This naturally brought them considerable advantages and as they had never mentioned it to him they did not even have the trouble of thanking him. This fear came to him especially at night. At times it almost drove him mad. Fortunately, in the morning, he realized that he had simply been the victim of his own imagination. However, his actions showed the results of these anxieties. More and more he tried to forestall them. 'Carry on as if I did not exist,' he used to say when he had given his advice about something, since the thought that someone might make use of it without his knowledge was so painful to him. It was as if what he held most dear was being taken from him and he could not even complain. At about two in the morning he put out the light. Emily was asleep. It always surprised him that she slept so well. He could hear the constant sound of her breathing. She slept like the young. He could speak, turn over, get up or walk about and she would never wake up. If he had been dozing, as he woke he could still hear the same breathing, not the sound of someone resting, but of someone struggling. Emily's exertions lasted all night, without wearying. 'How petty I am!' murmured Lesca. 'What does it matter to me if people make use of my advice? I'm not expecting anything to come of it, and yet I suffer as if I was expecting something. It's extraordinary how one must always shield oneself, against the world, against oneself, against everything.' Encouraged by the darkness he gradually began to feel resentment against Madame Maze. 'That woman is ridiculous. She does it on purpose to annoy me. If that's the case, everything must have been settled for a long time between her and her husband. It's not that I am making fun of Emily, it's Gabrielle who is making fun of me.' Then, suddenly judging what had happened more perceptively, he told himself that Madame Maze must certainly have been struck by his arguments and that she would be on the point of taking action, but without telling him. Once again he was lost in dark imaginings. 'It's appalling, it's all appalling. I seem like a crook. That's really what it is. She doesn't trust me. She doesn't want to get me mixed up in her affairs. She's right. I'm the one who's an idiot. All I had to do was not get mixed up in this business. And I go and get annoyed and make a tragedy of everything. Anybody would think I was personally involved.'

At last he could bear it no longer. He put the light on again. The effect on him was like a glass of water to a man dying of thirst. For several moments he looked at it wide-eyed. Eventually he got up. He took the precaution of closing Emily's bedroom door. It was half past three. He often got up like that in the middle of the night. He liked the surrounding silence and the little blue gas flames standing up in a circle on which he heated his coffee. He dressed and looked for a packet of cigarettes. He walked round his room for more than half an hour. Then he took some paper and a pencil and sat down. It had sometimes happened that he had written letters on behalf of other people, especially during the war. He had never seen any harm in it then. He had had the feeling he was doing a service as he made up elegant sentences. That night it was quite different. It seemed to him that in the act of imagining what somebody else ought to be saying there was something ugly, deceptive and hypocritical. He sat still for a while, thinking. The house and street were quite quiet. Only Emily's snores disturbed the silence. He wrote:

You will be surprised to receive this letter.

My dear Paul, my dear Pierre, my dear Jean.

You must certainly have thought you would never have any more news of me.

For my part, I thought I should never give you any.

When I left, I was full of illusions, etc.

I left you everything that belonged to me.

In my suffering, I was not thinking about such things. Many years have passed since then. You must have been able to see that my lack of interest was not an act, that it was deep and sincere. Now that we are now no longer even a separated couple, or divorced, but actually strangers to each other, I am asking you to put our affairs in order, so long as that would not be a nuisance to you at the moment. There is nothing in this request to cause you offence, you must understand. Equally there is nothing to humiliate me. During all these years I have not given a thought to what I was leaving behind me. Today, we are reasonable, aren't we?

We regret everything we have lost, spoilt, neglected, our youth as well as the rest.

We thought we were not clinging to anything. We were clinging to everything.

I am in no more need of what I left you today than I was before. But as everything is over, each one for himself, don't you think? Things ought to be in the right place.

As he read through this letter, or rather this rough draft, Lesca's eye-lid began to quiver. He looked at the time. It was half past five. He had taken two hours to write those few lines. He became aware that he was shivering with cold. He stood up. He was stiff all over. He began to walk about, taking short steps in order to increase the amount of movement. The skin of his face was so taut that it felt as if someone were pushing his eyelids apart. He felt dirty, old and worn out. The smell of fresh sweat mingled with the old smell of his clothes. So he was beginning to write letters for people who had not even asked him to! While he was at it, he had only to sign them too. He was filled with self-loathing. He really must have fallen pretty low to have got to that point. To write a letter like that to a man he had never seen! Out of kindness? Out of pity? Of course. But how unbecoming it was!

He went suddenly into Emily's room. She was sleeping with an obstinate expression on her face, as if she knew that it was light but did not want to wake up.

He touched her on the shoulder.

'I can't sleep, Emily,' he said.

She opened her eyes. He looked at her humbly, with great joy, uncomfortably like the way in which he had seen Olivetti look at him the day before. Emily sat up abruptly in bed, as if she had been caught out in some misdemeanour, and raised her head. She rather prided herself on attaching no importance to sleep or food, or to any of the needs of her poor old body. Lesca looked at her. Although she was a woman and no hair had grown on her cheeks in the night, he saw that she was as faded as he. There was no distinction between her lips and the surrounding flesh. Their skin was no longer smoother and more deeply coloured. He noticed underwear strewn about everywhere. He turned away his head. He dared not look at her.

'How happy I am to see you!' he said, still imitating Olivetti without being aware of it. 'I'll bring you some coffee, Emily. I should like you to talk to me. I didn't sleep last night and my head is so full of gloomy thoughts that I need someone here, awake, beside me.'

She took the cup of coffee he brought her, stooping over her attentively. He sat down next to the divan.

'I couldn't sleep. I heard midnight strike, one o'clock, two o'clock, three, four . . . It was frightful.'

Emily was drinking very slowly. She nodded her head occasionally, very quickly. She was not completely awake.

'It was because of you,' he went on.

She handed her cup to Lesca.

'Yes, it was because of you. You said such unfair things to me.'

She seemed not to hear.

'I know you were angry. I know you are sorry, but, in the dark, they worried me. I wondered if you might not be right. After all, perhaps you were right. I was selfish. I've never loved anyone. You see now you can hurt someone without meaning to when you are angry.'

Emily looked at her brother wearily.

'Please,' she said, 'don't begin making fun of me again. You didn't even listen to what I said. And the little you did hear has made no impression on you at all.'

Lesca made a startled movement.

'There really was no need,' continued Emily, 'to wake me up to tell me that.'

Lesca raised his arms as if in despair of making his sister understand.

'But that wasn't why I woke you up,' he cried. 'So you don't feel anything! You don't see anything!'

Emily closed her eyes, as if she were going to sleep again.

'So I am a stone? You think there is nothing here.'

He put his hand on his chest.

'Emily, please, listen to me, open your eyes. I can't wait. Say something. I need to hear something.'

Her eyelids lifted.

'What do you want me to say?' she asked. 'Tell me, tell me. I'll say it so you will leave me in peace.'

Lesca straightened up.

'Wait,' he cried, 'it won't be as long as you think. Then you will understand what I am. You belong to that wretched category of people who need to see in order to understand. Well, you will see, I promise, I solemnly promise. You will see, and you will understand, and you will be sorry. You are forgetting too many things. You think everything is all right for you, that I am defenceless, a poor wretch.'

Emily had closed her eyes again, but it was no good her pretending not to hear anything for a slight contraction of the corner of her mouth removed all repose from her face.

'Remember what I'm saying, Emily. This won't last. One day people will know what I am, you as well as the others. And people will be astonished. I never loved anyone . . . That's really something to laugh about. I, never to have loved anyone! I, a greedy, stony-hearted . . .'

He was in such a state of excitement that Emily got out of bed. She quickly put on a wrap and, taking her brother by the arm, pulled him into the other room.

'Calm down,' she said. 'You'll have an attack. Go to bed. You must rest.'

As soon as she had spoken these words, he was filled with peace. He looked at his sister with deepest gratitude.

'Yes, yes, you are right,' he said.

He lay down fully dressed. She went to fetch his overcoat and covered him up. He watched her doing it, his eyes shining with happiness.

'That's it, that's it,' he said.

She put out the light. A few minutes later, he was asleep.

Maurice and Emily came from the Bordeaux area. Their father, who had had an important job near Noyon, had ettled in that town. He had married there as well. His wife had died when Maurice and Emily were seven and four years old respectively. They had grown up in the care of an elderly servant woman. Five years later, their father had been found dead in his office at the factory with a revolver beside him. A judicial enquiry had been set up by the public prosecutor.

Although it was not good, the engineer's situation had not warranted such an act. The day before his suicide, a great many people had met him. He had never been seen by so many. Everyone agreed that he had been very cheerful. Two days earlier he had even been to see a property-owner in the town because he very much wanted one of his houses. Experts in these matters know that such an attitude is quite common in a man who has decided to kill himself. But ordinary people could not believe it was a suicide. In the end the business was closed, then forgotten, but still something of a mystery remained connected with the name of Lesca. The two children were taken in by a sister of Madame Lesca's, a woman of thirty-four, married but separated, who had been marked for life by something which had happened to her when she was young. When she was eighteen, she had been raped by a farm-worker employed by her parents. Nobody knew about it. She had grown older with the feeling of having been horribly dirtied. When she was thirty she had fallen in love with a man and married him. She had given him to understand that some dreadful misadventure had happened to her without clarifying it any further. A few months after the wedding she had confessed the truth. He did not seem worried by this admission. Nevertheless, three years later, he wanted a divorce and left her. A little while before, she had had a child, who had been still-born. This event upset her very deeply. She saw a connection between it and the dreadful thing that had happened to her. She was in such a state of mind that, when her sister's death occurred, followed by the still more tragic death of her brother-in-law, she was no longer in any doubt that some evil fate was pursuing her. It was only the fear of public censure that made her take the care of the orphans upon herself. Privately she thought she was not good enough for them. She did not feel strong enough to bring them up. She happened to be at a point in her life when she felt the need to turn in on herself rather than to find ways of branching out. However, she crushed these feelings and devoted herself entirely to the two children. But, despite all her good intentions, they were enveloped in a sad atmosphere. They were well aware that they were a burden to their aunt. She never spoke harshly to them, but there was something artificial in her affection. She was afraid of hurting them. She dared not oppose their wishes but at the same time was fearful that they would abuse their freedom. When he was eighteen, Maurice left to continue his studies in Paris. The separation from his sister, who was then fifteen, was painful. During the past few years, a deep friendship had grown up between the two young people. They agreed that they would meet again in Paris as soon as Emily was old enough to leave Noyon. Maurice had just finished his medical studies when Emily joined him. He had become a man. He had made many friends among the well-off students and when he saw his sister, plainly dressed, wearing a big hat on the back of her head, not at all pretty, in no way a credit to him, he was afraid that she would contradict the impression he wished to give of himself. As far as was possible, he kept her at a distance. Then, when he realized with some surprise that no one noticed anything out of the ordinary in the girl, he began to be jealous. He isolated her more and more. He stopped her seeing people who would have been very suitable friends for her. It was a difficult day for him when Professor Peix, thinking it would please him, offered to see what he could do for her. In the end he managed to settle her at Versailles, in a family he had known since his arrival in Paris and of whom he had no expectations. He used to go and see her from time to time. He was extremely kind now that he had nothing more to fear from her. Eventually she had come to understand what had been going on in her brother's mind. When she had arrived in Paris, she had been dreaming of a profound union between them. She had seen herself as collaborating with her brother (who would have become a great scholar), as his counsellor and friend. She had gone on hoping for two years. In the darkest moments there had always been a kind word to restore her courage. Finally, when she no longer doubted that she was deluding herself, she made the decision to shape her own life. She took a course in childcare. And, imperceptibly, she detached herself from her brother. It was at this time that he married Professor Peix's daughter. Convinced that he was heading for an outstanding position, he no longer gave any thought to his sister. Nevertheless, a few years later, he tried to see her again. A great change had taken place in him. It had not taken him long to realize that he had taken a false step. Coming young and green from the provinces, he had allowed himself to be dazzled by the Peix family and intimate conversations with the professor. The professor had a particular talent for initiating them in such a way that they seemed to be an immense favour. He used to speak about his son-in-law's future glory as if there were no doubt of it. Maurice listened with glowing admiration. He was ready to do anything people told him. He felt himself as yet incapable of pleasing except by showing complete good will and agreeing all the time. But very soon beneath those fine words he discovered a man of the type who holds forth to younger people, finding there the esteem he is always seeking. He became aware that the professor was as stupid as his daughter. He had imagined himself launched into Parisian society. He had imagined himself a fashionable doctor, still young, pleasing in his person, with connections, and so on. But behind the professor's great reputation there was nothing, neither intelligence, nor fortune, nor goodness, nor nobility. He was wearing himself out simply in order to make his own way and keep up appearances. He was hoping his son-in-law would be of assistance to him rather than thinking of giving him assistance. His young wife was struggling on everyone's behalf and was even more eager when it concerned her own family. The professor was a man of no real worth, weak, paralysed by a wife who felt obliged to maintain a position all the time. Maurice realized that he would not achieve anything in those surroundings, that he would never be anything but the little favourite of an ambitious family. He had only one wish left: to recover his freedom. When he had managed this, and it was more difficult than he could ever have imagined, he could see that, just as he had been mistaken in thinking that he was making an advantageous marriage, he had also been mistaken in devoting himself to medicine. He realized that he had no real vocation. Up to that point, all he had seen in his profession was a means of getting rich. He was thirty-three. What else could he do without money? To become rich and powerful by means of medicine was impossible as soon as he became aware that he had no vocation. Like Professor Peix, he would have had to put on airs all the time, to insinuate himself everywhere, to show an ability he did not possess. Then there began for Maurice that mediocre life of a man who has given up and who, because he cannot do anything else, continues on the very path which, deep down, he has given up. He kept on telling himself that it was temporary, that as soon as an opportunity appeared he would leave everything, but it lasted until the 1914 war. He founded a clinic in association with an elderly doctor who could not practise in his own name because of a conviction. Then he thought of his sister. He might be of use to her. But he had lost sight of her once again. He discovered her again with the help of his aunt in Noyon. She had married a petty official and lived in a two-roomed flat behind the rue d'Alésia. He was appalled to see her in such an undistinguished position and so proud of her child, whom she took for a walk in Montsouris park every afternoon. The provincial air which had made him blush ashamed him less than how she appeared now: a housewife without youth or charm, steeped in the odour of a very modest household. At that period he went to see her several times. He perceived at once that she would not agree to become involved with anything outside her home. Nevertheless he talked to her about the clinic. She never gave him a straightforward answer. He realized that her husband was giving her advice. He was a man of few resources who made no distinction between people except whether they were honest or dishonest. Maurice realized that in his eyes he belonged to the latter category and soon did not return. It had not taken the clinic long to go bankrupt. It was one of those businesses that often crop up, modelled on others that prosper, but which do not succeed themselves. Maurice became aware that it was not enough to take wise decisions. Circumstances had to be favourable too. He had believed he was acting bravely and intelligently when he had broken with middle-class surroundings and, ten years later, more and more regrets crowded in on him. The years were passing in such a way that at the end of each one he was no further forward. Never, despite all his efforts, had he found the means of living in the way he wanted. Always he had been waiting for an opportunity, while he scraped a living as best he could, without paying any attention to the passing of time. He was forty-two when the 1914 war broke out. He was called up with the rank of lieutenant-major. With the exception of a few incursions into the battle zone he spent the whole war in the South-West. For three months he found himself under the command of Professor Peix. His daughter was not mentioned. Although they were some fifteen years older, both of them were in fact at the same point. This produced rather a strange result. Lesca began to feel liking and respect for that same professor whom he had thought an imbecile. 'After all, Professor Peix isn't just anybody,' he thought. During the preceding years, because he had been living among insignificant people, the figure of the professor had come to mean more to him without his knowing it. He had to acknowledge that he was someone. Doctor-in-charge of the hospitals, officer of the Légion d'honneur, professor in the Medical School, such a personage would have created a sensation in the circles in which Lesca had been moving. If he had been at the head of the clinic, for example, bankruptcy would certainly have been avoided. The professor was aware of all this. He was very flattered. He was particularly considerate to the lieutenant-major, never alluding to the past or making his former son-in-law feel what he had lost through his own fault. When peace was restored, Lesca returned to Paris. He could open a consulting room again, especially as he was no longer at an age when a lack of funds makes movement impossible. He could hide his pre-war mistakes behind the war itself. But the mediocrity of the thing disgusted him. It would have been too stupid.

For some months he waited for he knew not what. He was going through a very galling time. He could see the small amount of money he had dwindling away. He had the impression that he would never earn any more, that he was being kept away from the progress shared by everyone else. The failure of his life became clearer and clearer. He was overwhelmed with regrets. A thousand details showed him the widening gap between the man he was and the man he had wished to be. He began to hunt out what he had despised or neglected before. Certain small daily events assumed enormous importance in his eyes. He no longer trusted anyone. The slightest opposition threw him into a rage. He could not make a new acquaintance without thinking in advance of the trouble it would bring him. One fine day, he felt the need to bestir himself and get out of this wretched condition. He needed a change, a place where he could rest and not bother about anything any longer. He seized upon the idea of going to stay with his sister for a while. He appeared at her house one morning, as usual without warning, as if he had left her the day before. The child had become a tall young man. When the family realized what a state Maurice was in, their former suspicion vanished. They could not do enough to be pleasant to Lesca. There is no one more charitable to the discouraged and the failures than unassuming people. Emily and her husband thought that Lesca had at last understood what they themselves had understood long before. They interpreted his wish to live with them as a tacit approval of their way of life and a criticism of his own. Now that he was a man like everybody else and had no more of those ambitions which are so humiliating for those who have none and was apparently satisfied with his lot, they could show him what they really were. But at the end of the month Lesca could no longer bear the atmosphere of jealousy and envy which, in order to please his hosts, he had to pretend to take for great virtue. Besides, they had grown bolder. They frowned when he went out. If he came back late, a chill hung over the meal. They had the impression that he had things to do, that he had not given up and that he was making preparations of some sort. One day, without being aware of the effect it was producing, he announced that he had met a very old friend (he meant his former colleague). 'I see you haven't changed!' observed Emily's husband sourly. Another day, he talked of going away for a few days to Noyon. 'If you don't like it with us, you mustn't feel obliged to stay!' they pointed out. Lesca went away a few days later to visit Noyon, but he did not go back to the rue d' Alésia. He was feeling better. His stay with his sister seemed less dismal. His aunt's house had been pulled down. He would be able to get some money by busying himself with war damages. There and then he obtained some increased allowances, a right to early payment, etc. He managed to get hold of some accommodation bills. And, which was no mean achievement, he made himself familiar with the new legislation, to such an extent that afterwards, by doing for other inhabitants of Noyon what he had done for his aunt, he was able to make quite a bit of money. But that spring soon ran dry. He had remained in contact with the professor. He had come to think that, in spite of everything, the man was more intelligent than most. He was amazed that, after what had happened, he had never borne him any grudge and that now, when he could have gloated over his lowly position, he continued to treat him as he had done when he had been showing the greatest promise. And then he also had to consider society. A connection of that sort, whether it was kept hidden or not, restored the confidence of a man whose station was no longer very clear.

He had to live. What was he to do now? In spite of his horror of everything connected with medicine, Lesca had to resort to it again, as he had been obliged to do all his life. He entered the service of a certain Doctor Chouard, a urinary specialist in the avenue Trudaine, but in a manner which in certain respects suited him fairly well. There was no question of his having to treat the patients, as the specialist kept this noble task for himself. His was an altogether more delicate job. The specialist had noticed that most of his clients maintained that the people who had contaminated them were not ill. They were above suspicion. How could they have been ill, etc. Doctor Chouard would then laugh sceptically. At that moment Lesca would appear, in a white overall as if he had been disturbed in the middle of some work in the laboratory. The specialist repeated what the patient had just said. It was then Lesca's turn to appear sceptical. The patient grew worried. When he had only a light attack, he began to be afraid of other more serious dangers. 'If this person is unwilling to come and see me,' said Doctor Chouard, 'if it would make things easier, my colleague could try to find out what's what. He could go with you and speak to this person.' That was when Lesca's task began. He took off his white overall, put on his jacket, picked up his hat and then went off with the patient. Often he had to wait in a café until the latter had prepared the way for his visit. Once he was in the presence of the presumed invalid, his task was to make use of all the resources of tact and psychology and gently persuade the person to go to the avenue Trudaine. If he pressed the point, he used to say, it was for a noble end. Fortunately, almost always, the people who thought they had nothing wrong with them had in fact nothing wrong. But the rare occasions when they were mistaken made all his trouble worthwhile. It was not right to risk ruining one's health, etc., when it was so simple for the matter to be settled once and for all. Often Lesca was asked to leave. But often too people let themselves be influenced by his inoffensive and good-natured air. Having thus increased the number of Doctor Chouard's patients by one unit, all he had to do was to wait for the settlement of the fees, when what was owed was paid to him punctually. It must be said that, two or three months before he had given himself over to this strange occupation, a curious phenomenon had taken place in Maurice Lesca's mental faculties. Although he had not grown noticeably older (he had put on a bit of weight, it is true), although he did not drink and had no vices, and although no misfortune had befallen him, he no longer wanted to think. His face had not changed. It was only when someone asked him a question that was too precise that this strange wish became perceptible. The centre of his gaze began to tremble, as a precision instrument might when somebody passed near it. Lesca did not reply. He knew nothing. He did not want to know anything. Why were people asking him questions? Couldn't they leave him in peace?

One day Lesca received a letter from his sister. Her husband had died suddenly. Yet he had not been ill. In the morning he had gone to the office as usual. At midday the baker's wife had come up to pass on a telephone message from the firm of Crespin. Emily's husband was not feeling well. He would not be back for lunch. At three o'clock there was another message. He wanted his wife to come and fetch him. She hurried round at once. She found her husband sitting on a chair, surrounded by four or five colleagues. He smiled when he saw her. In the offices work was continuing. Nevertheless she was alarmed at his appearance. Lines of shadow made his features stand out. He had unbuttoned his collar. There was something youthful about his bared neck. He was incapable of replying to the questions everyone was asking him. He did not know what was the matter with him. When he was asked where the pain was, he raised his hand to show that he did not know. Emily took him back home. He went to bed as soon as he arrived. Perhaps he ought not to have done, for scarcely was he lying down and

47

covered up, when he suffered a brief heart-failure, which was soon followed by another. At midnight he was dead. Emily had fought against the stupidity of this misfortune. She tried to obtain some clarification. She was astounded to learn, from the mouth of the very doctor who, a few hours earlier, had told her there was nothing to worry about, that her husband had been seriously ill for years. It was incredible. He had never complained. He had never even considered consulting a doctor. She could still remember his fear, every time he had to go before a review board, that his myopia might not be enough to maintain his status as one who had been invalided out of the army. She remembered that he had complained that Crespin's had kept back a certain amount of money in case of sickness, and also that on numerous occasions when he had needed an excuse for not going to the office he had never dreamed of saying it was on account of the state of his health.

Lesca did not answer his sister's long letter. But a few weeks later he sent her a money order. It was the first of a long series. She thanked him. She asked him to come and see her or else, if it was not possible for him to travel, to let her know where she could meet him. Again he did not reply. A little while afterwards, he sent her another money order. She wrote to him immediately, sending him further details about her life, about what she planned to do, and about what she hoped and expected of her son. She imagined that the money orders were the proof of the great interest her brother felt in her. No doubt he was sorry that he had not always behaved towards her as he ought. She hid nothing of her life from him and gave him to understand that all that was forgotten and he could be quite comfortable about it. He still did not reply, but sent another money order. She wrote to him, without thanking him this time, to tell him how she was using the money. It was as if she were unwilling to display her feelings of gratitude. She did not really understand what lay behind this mysterious way of helping her. She was intrigued. Certain things her husband had said came back to her. Once again she received a money order. Lesca had not found a single word to write in the place for correspondence, even though it was so small. She replied once more, for the last time. None the less, Lesca went on sending her money. He never thought about her.

Suddenly, as he passed a post office, he would go in, join the queue for money orders, fill in a form, hand over the money, put the receipt in his wallet, and, when he came out, he would experience a feeling of immense well-being. This would last for a week, or a fortnight, until the time when once again, in order to recover it, Lesca would go into a post office. As long as he remained with Doctor Chouard, he sent money in this way. But nine months later he left. He then no longer had the means to send money orders. At first he suffered from this as if from some physical deprivation. Then he grew used to it. At this time Emily sent him several letters. When he recognized his sister's writing, he did not open them and put them in a drawer. It was not until much later on, at a time when new prospects were opening before him and he was considering sending money to his sister again, that he opened them. Emily was astonished at the way he was behaving. She asked him to send her some money by return of post, as she counted on it. If he had not wished to send any more, he might at least have warned her. She told him that he was arrogant and boastful, that he had been making fun of her, that he had no real kindness, that he had been trying to humiliate her and that, having achieved his aim, he had revealed his true nature. Lesca displayed no bitterness. He tore up the letters. He had other preoccupations. The new prospects were more interesting. He had seen his former colleague again. There was a scheme to set up not a clinic but a nursing home, on the outskirts of Paris. The capital had already been collected. Lesca could be useful because of his connection with Professor Peix. All that was being asked of him was to persuade the professor to agree to be the chairman of the management committee. Lesca was introduced to several people. He did not notice that, given his modest part, there were far too many introductions. 'And what about me?' asked Lesca, when he learned that all the doctors belonging to the establishment were to be shareholders. 'It's up to you to come to some arrangement with the professor,' replied his friend. 'As you are obtaining such a splendid position for him, ask him to enable you to become one of us in exchange.' He gave Lesca some advice. The main thing was not to seem to be asking the professor for a favour, but on the contrary to seem to be doing him one.

Lesca did not flinch. He went to see his former father-in-law. But the latter, however Lesca might insist, refused, on the pretext that he was too old (he was nearly seventy-eight). Lesca thought all was lost but then Professor Peix, with that air of indifference assumed by people who always have their own interests at heart even when they apparently no longer do, said to him: 'And my son-in-law, Professor Paluel, wouldn't he do just as well as I would at the head of your committee?' The sleeping partners pretended to be disappointed, then they accepted. So it was that Lesca came to make the acquaintance of the man who had married his wife. The interview took place at Professor Peix's house. At no time did Lesca display the least uneasiness. Even though, in spite of the importance of the conversation, Professor Paluel was secretly watching Lesca whenever the opportunity offered, the latter did not even seem to know in whose presence he was. The business was arranged. It was even decided when it was to be put into effect. Then it came to grief. Legal proceedings were initiated. A few weeks later, Professor Paluel was surprised to learn that part of the amount he had deposited on behalf of Lesca (a very small part, it is true) had been repaid to the latter by the authorities. Lesca had never mentioned it! Professor Paluel told the story to his father-in-law. They decided to wait for Lesca's explanation. It was so confused and incoherent that within a few minutes Paluel's attitude towards Lesca had changed completely. He began to laugh. In his eyes Lesca no long existed. He was an eccentric, a sick man, unsettled, who did not know what he was doing. 'You wouldn't believe me. I've always told you so,' commented Professor Peix as soon as Lesca had gone out.

A short while after these extraordinary events, Lesca became seriously ill. For a month beforehand he had noticed that, as soon as he had finished washing, as if contact with water alone had been enough, an unbearable headache developed. He no longer dared to wash. For two or three days he felt better. Then simply having his breakfast brought on those appalling headaches. He went without it. In order to escape the pain, he thought, he would need ideal conditions. No noise, no effort, no shocks, and above all no emotional strain. Then he tried to find these ideal conditions but, as it was impossible, he kept on getting angry. People wanted to kill him. Everybody was conspiring against him, and so on. Then his condition grew worse. One morning he woke up trembling with fear. It had just become clear to him that even ideal conditions would not be enough.

He had just woken up. He had not heard any noise, nor experienced any emotion, and yet he had an appalling pain in his head. Nothing had happened and he was already ill. Then, in addition to the headaches, he soon developed a state of constant feverishness. Sometimes he used to go home at three o'clock in the afternoon in order to go to bed. The mere act of taking off his hat made him shiver. This lasted for a month and, suddenly, one evening he became delirious. His temperature was one hundred and four degrees. He called out. The hotel chambermaid went to tell Professor Peix. He was in bed. He telephoned his son-in-law who hurried round at once and himself took Lesca to the Laënnec Hospital in his own car. For six weeks it was impossible to bring his temperature down. His heart, which was already weak, sometimes could not be heard when it was sounded. A fatal outcome seemed imminent, when suddenly, one morning, the fever subsided. Lesca was saved. He went to convalesce for a few months in a sort of medical hotel in the Midi which was managed by somebody Professor Paluel knew. It was when he returned to Paris that he settled in the rue de Rivoli. Faced with the severity of his condition, the family in Bordeaux had sent him a small sum of money. Thanks to Professor Paluel's kindness, he had had no need to spend it. Then was the beginning of a gloomy existence for Lesca. The illness had completely changed him. He had given up any kind of activity. The little money his family had given him vanished rapidly. He had the sympathy, though it was rather hard to understand, of Professor Peix and of Paluel. When he went to ask them for a small kindness, they rarely refused him.

He had been scraping along like that for five years when one morning someone knocked at his door. It was Emily, but how much she too had changed. Her petit bourgeois look had vanished. There was a certain rigidity about her. She carried an enormous wicker suitcase. She had climbed the four storeys with that case without knowing whether her brother was there

51

or if he would be able to let her stay. Lesca helped her bring in her case. She sat down at once. A few minutes later she raised her eyes and saw her brother. He had changed. She did not notice. That was how she moved in with him. She never gave him any reason. However he eventually came to realize that something had happened between her and her son.

Lesca stopped a few paces from Madame Maze's shop. He drew his wallet from his pocket, opened it warily as it had the fragments of so many old papers in it, and made sure that the letter – or rather, the draft – he had written during the night was safely there. Then, for the space of half a minute, with his head high and looking straight ahead of him, he breathed deeply.

The bookshop had a counter covered with books, a bit like the counter in a chemist's shop. Behind it, a sort of alleyway led to a dark back room. On the other side of that was Madame Maze's flat, first the living-room, then the bedroom. These two rooms had nailed-up windows which gave on to a narrow courtyard.

'Don't worry, it's me,' said Lesca, who had closed the street door very quickly in order not to activate the electric bell and gone straight behind the counter.

'I wasn't expecting you any longer. How is it that you are so late?' said Madame Maze, coming hastily to meet him.

Lesca reddened slightly. He suddenly had the impression that Madame Maze did not trust him. It was ridiculous. But why had she come running? He looked at his watch, began by pretending to be surprised it was so late, then said he always came at that time. He went and sat down by an old gas heater with most of the asbestos elements broken. It was chilly in the two rooms. They must originally have been sheds. The curtains and the carpets covering the concrete floor merely looked warm.

While he was having his tea, Lesca hardly spoke at all. He felt strangely disturbed. He smiled in order to conceal it. He did not dare go so far as to say anything. Suddenly he said:

'I've got a letter for you, Gabrielle.'

52

'A letter!'

He took hold of it in his pocket without pulling out his wallet, like a formal document.

'It's a draft . . . a rough draft of a letter,' he stammered.

He dared not give it to her.

'Show me the letter,' said Madame Maze.

'No, no, I've been thinking. It's an idea I had. But it's a stupid idea.'

'As you have it there, give it to me. Come on, give it to me.'

He looked at Madame Maze angrily and then screwed up the paper.

'I tell you I don't want to show it to you.'

'But what is it about?' asked Madame Maze, suddenly worried.

'Oh, I'm sorry!' cried Lesca. 'If only you knew what was going on inside me. I'm so afraid of hurting you and, at the same time, I feel I can't do anything else if I want to protect you . . . protect you . . .'

'So it's about that business again?'

'Wait. Listen to me first. Sit down. I'll read it to you. You'll understand.'

He unfolded the paper, and looked at it for a long time. Then he began to tremble. Why had he not re-read the letter before he mentioned it? What was he getting mixed up in? What was the matter with him that he was taking someone else's interests so much to heart?

'No, no, no,' he cried.

He stood up abruptly and tore the letter in half.

'So what was in the letter?' asked Madame Maze, going up to him and looking him in the eye.

'There were ideas, ideas that came to me in the night. You are right, Gabrielle. You are right to think that I am meddling in what does not concern me. You are absolutely right.'

He fell silent. Drops of sweat formed on the end of his nose. He kept wiping them off, but they re-appeared immediately.

'And what if all that was play-acting!' he burst out suddenly. 'If everything was happening according to a plan, and there was no letter, if I had been pretending not to want to give it to you, if I had been pretending to want to read it, if I had known

53

beforehand that I was going to tear it up . . . That's what you are thinking, aren't you?'

He passed a hand over his face from forehead to chin several times in succession.

'But what was in the letter then?' insisted Madame Maze.

'I can't tell you now. I shall never tell you. Why? Why? Why? Because there was no longer any doubt . . . All that would have been play-acting.'

He sat down again. Taking advantage of the fact that Madame Maze was looking at him, as she wondered what was the matter with him, he said in a voice grown calm and serious:

'Let's talk about something else, Gabrielle, shall we?'

Then, in the artificial tone of somebody changing the subject, he added:

'What was the weather like today? Did it rain or not?'

'Now you really are play-acting, Maurice. Come on, tell me what your letter was about.'

He closed his eyes and covered them with his hand. The lower part of his face contracted, as if it were hiding too.

'I am not happy, Gabrielle,' he murmured. 'I have a strong feeling that you don't really understand what I want. Besides, it's my fault and that makes me sad too. I wanted you to write a letter. The only reason I have for wanting that is for your benefit. But as soon as it is a matter of benefit, I don't know any longer, everything gets confused, everything is possible . . . and I, with my poor feelings, I don't know what to say or do any longer. I take fright. If you, Gabrielle, if you could . . . I dare not say what . . . And even now . . . I'm talking to you . . . But if everything I was saying wasn't sincere . . . even now . . . if I was play-acting . . .'

Again and again Madame Maze smote her hands together.

'Maurice, Maurice, come on, come on . . . that's enough.'

He bowed his head. The noise of clapping had been extremely disagreeable to him, but he did not want to show it for fear of annoying Madame Maze.

'Yes, it's enough,' he said, so that she should not start clapping again.

At the same moment, his eye began to quiver.

'Gabrielle,' he murmured as he held her hands, 'what do you think of me?'

'Why?'

'I don't know. It seems to me that you don't understand.'

'Yes, I do, much better than you think.'

'No, you don't understand.'

His face wore a mournful expression. He squeezed Madame Maze's hands and leaned towards her.

'The thing is, I love you, Gabrielle.'

He had scarcely uttered the words when he began to cough.

Madame Maze stood up and went to fetch him a drink.

'I love you,' he repeated. 'You are my only friend.'

He turned as if someone had been coming in, assumed the expression of a madman, then recomposed his features. There was nobody.

'You really believe, Maurice, that I ought to do it?'

Lesca jumped, then he was filled with an immense joy. He hunched his shoulders and screwed up his eyes against the light which was pouring over his face.

'What are we really, Gabrielle?' he said. 'We are the victims of our own illusions.'

'I sometimes wonder. It's true,' said Madame Maze.

Lesca looked at her severely. Her eyes were lowered. She could not see him. For a moment or two Lesca scowled. Suddenly Madame Maze looked at him. He was perturbed, then his lips lengthened and narrowed. It was impossible to say whether this strange expression was the ghost of a smile or an indication that he felt like crying.

'I really didn't want to ask him for anything,' said Madame Maze. 'He was so ill-natured and churlish. I felt it was the only way I had of punishing him.'

Lesca raised his arms and shook them frenziedly. He seemed like a man who was so sure of being in the right that he would rather die on the spot than be silent.

'Oh!' he cried. 'That's madness. How can you believe that? Oh, how can you be so stupid!'

He stopped suddenly, aware that he had gone too far. But, in spite of this vehemence, Madame Maze had not flinched. Raising his voice still further, he went on:

'The only way of punishing him! The only way of punishing him! Little he cares. What do you expect punishments like that to do to him? I ask you, Gabrielle. Heavens, what innocence! You are wonderful, Gabrielle. You are wonderful. You are still a child. You have a child's illusions.'

Madame Maze was gently stroking her hair with her fingertips. It was not yet possible to tell what she was going to say. She was not thinking. She was suffering because she felt what Lesca was saying was true and also because what she had done was right. So what she had taken for something fine was in fact stupidity! She could not yet believe it. But Maurice was right. She had been stupid. It was only weak-minded people who thought it possible to be both at the same time. Her face was growing more and more melancholy. Lesca noticed it. He spoke a few incoherent words. Then he addressed her. He was sorry for her. He had been too hard on her. He had not thought she would have been so easily crushed. He had wounded her.

'I'm sorry,' he said, suddenly gentle. 'You are the one who is right, Gabrielle. You did a fine thing and what I am doing is ugly.'

She raised her eyes. He was watching her carefully, with the attention of a man who attaches no importance to what he is saying. It did not even occur to him to put more sincerity into his look. It was too serious a moment for the hypocrisy of everyday relationships to be needed.

'Never again shall I speak to you about this business,' he went on as gently as before. 'Everyone ought to act in this life as he thinks fit. Everyone knows better than his neighbour what is right for him. And everything we do which goes against our own deep feelings, if we allow ourselves to be influenced, for example, will one day tell against us. You were unselfish! That is excellent. You must be like that. You are generous and proud! That is excellent.'

Lesca paused, out of breath.

'I think so too,' said Madame Maze, evidently happy at his words.

Lesca felt a tearing pain inside him. He went on as if nothing was the matter.

56

'Yes, it's the only reasonable thing. We make light of our own interests, don't we, Gabrielle? There are so many beautiful things in life! How happy we should be if we were free! Gabrielle, for years you have obeyed your instincts. Carry on with it, carry on, remain yourself and you will never regret anything.'

'It's better like that, isn't it?'

'Much better, infinitely better. Now, Gabrielle, I must ask something for myself. Forget what has happened. Tell me that you aren't angry with me.'

Madame Maze looked at him in astonishment.

'I ought not to have caused doubt in your mind,' Lesca went on. 'But you see, Gabrielle, it sickened me.'

He clasped his hands.

'I was only thinking of your good,' he continued. 'I should have realized that no one knows the true good of every individual, shouldn't I, shouldn't I?'

When he went out he was in a state of such excitement that he simply walked without thinking of going home. He did not even notice that he was going past the little street which led to the embankments and which he usually took. 'I've stopped her accepting, I've stopped her accepting,' he repeated ceaselessly. 'It's splendid! Splendid!' He bumped into a passer-by. He turned furiously. 'You did that on purpose,' he cried. The man looked at him with such surprise that Lesca stammered out an excuse and ran away. 'It's splendid! Splendid!' At length he noticed that he was getting further away from where he lived. He retraced his steps. His excitement was beginning to fade. As his breathing was becoming difficult, he stopped to get back his breath. 'It's splendid,' he said, 'but I am no longer strong enough to get into such a state.' Gradually he began to consider more clearly what had just happened. Then he was amazed at the madness that had seized him when he left Madame Maze. And very slowly, as if he had been taking a little walk for the sake of his health, he went home.

Emily was doing some sewing. She must have been indulging in gloomy thoughts all afternoon because the look she gave her brother had nothing in common with the peaceful occupation with which she was busying herself. Lesca closed the door again without saying a word. He went into the kitchen but did nothing at all there. Shortly afterwards, he came out again. Emily had already gone back into her room. He joined her there. As usual, he was still wearing his hat and overcoat. He was holding an evening paper he had just bought. Emily did not even raise her head. He looked at what she was doing, although he was not in the least interested in it. He saw that she was hemming the bottom of a sleeve and was finding it very difficult to do without using up too much fabric.

'I'm sure that won't show,' he said.

She still did not raise her head. Experience had taught her not to fall into that trap.

'Aren't you afraid the sleeve may be too short?' he asked.

'It doesn't matter,' she said, carrying on with her small task with apparent concentration.

In fact it was of no more interest to her than it was to Lesca.

He began to prowl round the room. He was thinking about Madame Maze. The woman's story was a typically personal one, a story to which Madame Maze alone could attribute any importance. Everyone has episodes of this kind in life, so full of consequences for himself, so very insignificant for anyone else. 'And as for me, I am behaving as if this business meant as much to me as to Madame Maze!' He stopped walking. 'That's what's ugly,' he murmured. He knew that actually it did not matter to him whether Madame Maze tried to get back the money or not. What difference did it make to him? What was he getting mixed up in? Why was he making so much trouble for himself? For Madame Maze's sake? He began to laugh so noisily that Emily looked up.

'What's the matter with you?' she asked.

'What's the matter with me?' he said, not yet knowing what answer he was going to give.

He went on laughing.

'What's the matter with me?' he repeated. 'I'm happy, very happy. I suppose you're pleased, my dear Emily.'

Emily had realized that, as usual, she would not be able to get anything out of her brother. She busied herself with her work again.

'Listen to me, Emily.'

She pretended not to hear.

'I must explain something to you, something very important. Do you know what I want to talk about? I want to talk about the difference between what appears and what is.'

'Yes, I know,' said Emily, holding her work up so she could examine the whole thing.

'I am not what I seem to be,' said Lesca.

'I know, I know,' said Emily, bending her head to the left, then to the right.

'You'll soon see, Emily.'

This time, she looked at her brother.

'You are always saying that,' she said irritably. 'But what do you expect me to make of it? Once and for all, tell me. Are these threats?'

He turned abruptly. He liked having a discussion with someone who was sitting down. He would gesture repeatedly and make frequent turns. He would come and go.

'I'm telling you this because you seem not to understand certain things.'

'What things?'

He looked extremely surprised.

'You are asking me what things, you, Emily? Come on, you know very well what I mean.'

'Do I?'

'Yes. You'll see. Have a little patience. You'll understand.'

'I shall understand what?' she asked, restraining herself.

'The difference,' he replied softly, with an air of mystery.

This time she contented herself with shrugging her shoulders and then took up her work again. Lesca left the room. He took off his overcoat and his hat. For a short while he stood motionless, unsure what he ought to do. Then he went back to Emily.

'I forgot to tell you something.'

Emily closed her eyes wearily. He looked at her for some time, then, as if he had given up trying to make her see reason, he went out again. He wandered round his room for about ten minutes. He was thinking about Madame Maze. Yes, he had been right. It was not for him to give her advice. One ought never to force people to do what they do not want. However great his affection for Madame Maze, he ought to leave her free. He ought never even to have spoken to her about her husband.

'Emily!' he called suddenly.

'What do you want now?'

He went up to his sister. He was smiling. He was rubbing his hands.

'I am pleased with you,' he said.

She kept quiet.

'I have discovered something. It all comes from the state of my health. A few years ago I was not at all like this. You weren't here. You couldn't take it into account.'

Emily went on sewing as if she were alone.

'I repeat, Emily, I'm pleased with you. You're right to be as you are. You understood that it was difficult to be otherwise with me. You are absolutely right. The truth is that, at times, I don't really know what I'm doing any longer. Everything goes so badly. Everything is so hopeless.'

Emily raised her eyes.

'So you can't stop talking, Maurice.'

Lesca's face contracted. A cloud appeared before his eyes. So she thought that he was still joking. He opened his heart and was asked when he was going to be quiet. He was on the point of losing his temper when, suddenly, he murmured: 'Was I really speaking seriously?'

'You're right,' he said, for the sake of saying something.

Suddenly he sat down on the divan beside Emily.

'Emily,' he said, taking hold of her hands to prevent her from sewing.

She looked at him. He was not looking at her. He was staring intently just to one side of her. He stayed like that for a while, without saying a word, while Emily, who was somewhat fearful, kept perfectly still. Then he stood up and went back to his own room. 'I wasn't speaking any more seriously than before,' he thought as he walked to and fro. 'That is to say, it could have been the case that I was speaking seriously, but circumstances did not allow. Oh! let's think about something else.' He opened the window and closed the shutters. Then he went back into Emily's room to close hers too. It was the only thing he did for her. Because it was necessary to lean out in order to unhook the shutters, he was always afraid she might fall out of the window – a fear impossible to understand. But it never even occurred to him to cast a glance in his sister's direction.

As he went on his way in the direction of the rue Monge, Lesca enjoyed looking at the shops and the busy life of the streets. It was fine. The sky was blue. A few white clouds floated in the distance, but they were disappearing. Lesca walked slowly. When he stopped before a display, he did not seem like a prospective customer but like a man who is interested in things for their own sake. From time to time he raised a hand to his forehead, as if he wanted to check whether he was hot or cold. He felt calm. Why had he been so upset the day before? He wondered about it now and again. But he looked in vain for an answer to that question, he could not find one. He went along the boulevard Saint-Germain, instead of the rue des Ecoles as he usually did. Some children were playing in the Cluny gardens. He glanced briefly at the beggars' placards hung on the railings. Then he went on his way. Something under the ground was being built or repaired because, for a distance of a hundred yards or so, people had to walk on boards between some fencing and the railings of the gardens. Today the inconvenience amused him. There were places where he had to wait for other people to pass before it was his turn to go on. He waited endlessly and the people behind him grumbled. He dawdled along like this for more than half an hour. He did not like arriving at Madame Maze's before it was beginning to grow dark. That was why he preferred to go and see her in the winter. At last shadows were mingled with the light. It was still quite light, but he no longer felt reluctant to go and shut himself up in the back of a shop. Before he went in, he stopped for a moment, as people do when they have climbed several flights of stairs, not to get back his breath, but to think about Madame Maze. It was imperative for him to know where he was going and to recollect where he was in his relations with his dear friend. He pictured the inside of the shop and the rooms behind it. Finally, he went in. Madame

Maze was waiting for him as usual. He went behind the rack of books and along the little passage. Madame Maze greeted him with a delighted smile. She was wearing a dress made of silk foulard as soft and flowing as voile, but underneath she was wrapped up tightly like an invalid.

'You are punctual today,' she said.

He sat down without taking off his overcoat..

'Aren't you going to take off your coat?'

'Oh, I'm sorry! You're right.'

Since he had arrived at Madame Maze's, he had given the impression of being somewhat apprehensive. Madame Maze made the tea. Several times he turned round to see what she was doing. All of a sudden his eye began to quiver. He rubbed it and pressed on it with his forefinger.

'There's something strange about you,' said Madame Maze.

'No, no, there isn't,' replied Lesca.

'What's happened?'

'Nothing. I assure you. Nothing.'

He began to laugh. The day before he had laughed with Emily. He was laughing now. Nothing could be more natural. When he laughed one day, he could be certain that he would laugh again the next day and sometimes the day after that too. He got out of the easy chair in order to sit on an upright one.

'What's the matter with you, Maurice?' asked Madame Maze.

'Are you asking me that question because I prefer the upright chair to the armchair?'

'No, not particularly.'

'I need to be higher up. I don't know why. Perhaps because I feel tired.'

He began to laugh again.

'Have you thought about what happened yesterday?' asked Madame Maze suddenly.

He looked at her. Their eyes met as they had done on the day when they had first seen each other. He turned his head away immediately.

'No,' he said. 'Besides, it's over. There's no need to talk about it any more. We ought not to talk about it any more.'

'You're right, Maurice.'

As he had done the day before, he experienced a tearing pain. In order to conceal his agitation, he tapped the table with one finger after another.

'Come on,' he said, 'let's talk about something else.'

He had hardly spoken these words when his hand flew to his chest and at the same time he clutched at his waistcoat, tie and sweater.

'Oh, heavens!' cried Madame Maze.

'I don't know, I don't know,' he stammered.

The patch above his top lip was covered in drops of sweat.

'Are you feeling ill?' asked Madame Maze.

'I don't know,' he answered. 'I don't know yet.'

He was still gripping on to his clothes. Suddenly he leaned back in his chair. Then he let his head drop back. Madame Maze got up and tried to make him let go of his waistcoat.

'Leave me alone, leave me alone.'

His breathing was rapid and noisy. He straightened up and looked at Madame Maze.

'No, don't leave me,' he said.

He let go of his waistcoat and took hold of Madame Maze's hands which he squeezed as hard as before.

'Are you ill?' she asked.

'I don't know yet.'

'But if you aren't ill . . .'

'Be quiet,' he said, squeezing her more tightly.

From time to time he passed his tongue over his lip to remove the sweat. But he had it on his forehead now and all round his nostrils. There was sweat on his temples too, for his hair was damp.

'You frighten me, Maurice. Tell me what's the matter. Would you like a drink? Would you like to lie down?'

'Leave me, leave me.'

He did not let go of Madame Maze's hands. His eyes darted about, up and down as often as from left to right. Ordinarily, they were rather dim. That day they were bigger than usual and extraordinarily mobile. Suddenly he let go of Madame Maze's hands. He lowered his head very slowly, then raised it again. He put his hand on his chest again, but without clenching it, as if for a caress. His breathing was becoming more regular. He said:

'What was the matter with me, Gabrielle?'

'Nothing's the matter, you're better,' she replied.

'I wasn't in pain,' he said. 'I was frightened. I thought I was going to have a pain here.'

He pointed to his chest.

'It's the first time I have seen you in such a state.'

'Ah!' he said.

'You know quite well you have never been in this state before.'

He looked at the tea-pot and cups. Then he turned slightly.

'I'm getting better, I'm getting better. There's no doubt about it. I'll be able to tell you what the matter was soon.'

He drank a cup of tea, then stayed completely motionless for a while.

'Do you know what was the matter with me?' he asked, turning cautiously towards Madame Maze. 'A backlash. It was a backlash. Yesterday my nerves were on edge. And I didn't want to talk about that business any more. I was wrong, Gabrielle. Since then I have been thinking about lots of things. What do you think? Am I really wrong?'

'What?'

He put his hand on his chest again.

'I'm not ill,' he said. 'I wasn't ill. Listen to me, Gabrielle. I must talk to you. Oh, not about me, about you. I said one thing yesterday, then I said the opposite. Just now I thought I was wrong. What shall I be thinking in five mintues? The opposite of what I think now, no doubt. You know, Gabrielle, I am in the process of becoming another man. I suddenly have the impression that I'm going to feel a dreadful pain . . . and I feel nothing. I didn't feel anything just now, absolutely nothing, and yet you saw what a state I was in. And then, I have extraordinary doubts. All night I was wondering if you didn't despise me.'

'What an idea, Maurice!' cried Madame Maze.

'I don't know why. Or rather, I do know, but I can't explain it to you. There are moments, Gabrielle, when I have the impression that everything is abandoning me. In my madness I am completely incapable of keeping hold of the few people who care for me. I want to do everything and I don't know what. With you, that is what's happening at the moment. I feel

I'm right and then I tell myself I'm wrong. Now I don't know what else to say to you, Gabrielle. I can't give you any advice. And I go about things in such a way that, whatever you do, I shall be aware that I have done badly. It's unbelievable, but it's always like that.'

'You are still thinking about that business!'

'That business? Oh, no. I'm not thinking about that particularly. It's simply an illustration of a state of mind that is always the same in all circumstances. Fundamentally, I don't want to yield to the evidence, but perhaps my life is over.'

'Don't say such silly things.'

Lesca reddened.

'Don't think I really mean it,' he answered. 'My life is far from over. I shall do extraordinary things . . . wait and see. No, no, I'm saying something stupid. You are right again. I am saying silly things.'

Gabrielle went over to Lesca. She put a hand on his shoulder.

'Calm down, calm down. You are excited. It will all pass.'

He did not reply. He took her hand and stroked it. Abruptly, he stood up.

'Yes, yes,' he cried, 'let's be as we were before. Don't let's carry on like this. I know quite well it's all my fault.'

'You're not letting me speak,' said Madame Maze. 'I was going to tell you something that will please you.'

Lesca went pale. He glanced slyly at Madame Maze. Then he bowed his head to listen to what she was going to say.

'You are more intelligent than I am, Maurice, you are wiser. But, for better or worse, I am a woman. I acted like a woman. Thanks to you, my dear Maurice, I now see things more clearly.'

An immense happiness enveloped Lesca. He hid his face in his hands.

'No, no, no,' he cried. 'Don't let's talk about that any more. I don't want to hear it mentioned. It's appalling. The whole business is appalling. I believed one thing was right for you. Then I did not believe it any longer. Now it's over.'

A few days later Lesca was making his way along the boulevard des Italiens. It was ten o'clock in the morning. The weather was mild and damp. He walked without looking at anything. In the middle of the bustle of the city he gave the impression of being just as he was at home. From time to time he looked for a number above the porch of a house. But he was still a long way from the place where he was going, for as he did not find it he continued on his way as before. There was something novel in his bearing. That day he had a particular goal, as he used to have when he was engaged in business or was going to visit a patient. He seemed to be feeling a certain pride in himself, although he kept muttering: 'What impression am I giving? What impression am I giving?' He looked as if he were dressed in his Sunday best. Or rather he had looked like that when he left home, for now, by making all sorts of small adjustments, he was trying hard to lose the look. He had loosened his tie. He had turned up the collar of his overcoat. 'I don't care about them,' he murmured from time to time. 'But what am I going to look like? It's absurd. I wonder why I've got myself involved in this business.' He remembered Madame Maze and, all of a sudden, he reddened. What did she really think? She would have had to have been blind not to notice that he had suddenly changed, when, the other day, she had finally yielded. Although he might cry: 'No, no, no, it's dreadful', an immense joy had flooded over him. And when afterwards she had told him that all he had to do was to go and see her lawyer on her behalf, she could not have failed to see, in spite of his 'it's dreadful', that inwardly he was delighted. Why? Madame Maze might well ask. Am I not free to throw my money out of the window if I want to? Why does he attach so much importance to my not losing anything that belongs to me? Does he love me so much? Does he believe it so sincerely that he lays claim to my future? Is he really afraid that one day I may be in need? It's absolutely absurd. Everything Lesca undertook, even if its aim was quite unselfish, turned against him. And here he was today making his way to the boulevard Bonne-Nouvelle, to a notary he did not know, to talk about something he no longer had at heart. He had put on a stiff collar. What was he going to say? He did not even know. He had woken up too recently. And yet

66

he looked as if he was very much concerned in the affair . . .
'What do I look like?' he murmured. 'A man who leaves his
home at ten o'clock in the morning to go and see a notary.
Good heavens, how clumsy I am! I go about things in such
a way that I seem selfish, when in fact I have others' interests
at heart. Absurd, the whole thing is absurd.' Madame Maze
could not doubt that he had some ulterior motive. It was
shameful. Ought he not to have been firmer? Since Gabrielle
did not actually want the money, why cause so much bother?
And the attack? Might it not seem deliberate one day? 'I am a
wretched idiot! When I give a present I do it in such a strange
way that people hesitate to accept and wonder why I am
doing it. Oh, not Madame Maze! Not yet at any rate. She is
a kindly woman. She sees no harm in it. She has no friend to
point it out to her, except me. But one day, who knows?' He
continued on his way, still walking with youthful briskness
like an active man. 'Yes, what am I going to look like? What
is the old grey-beard doing in this business? The notary is sure
to wonder.' So Lesca was going to play the part of those people
he despised, people who claim to be authorized by others and
who prompt the question: 'What can they have done to earn
the trust of those they represent?' and whom people loathe
because it is harder to come to an understanding with them
than with the interested parties themselves.

Lesca cast an envious look at the office. The first room was
divided from the public by a railing like a royal chamber.
Furtively Lesca watched the clerks sitting behind small tables
and the walls lined with bound volumes of records. He
thought: 'It's a good business.' The chief clerk occupied the
middle of the room. He was sitting behind a real desk. He
asked for some information. A clerk responded immediately.
'I would have done better to follow that path,' said Lesca to
himself. He went over to a window dimmed by grime. It
looked on to a courtyard congested with box-tricycles and
handcarts, where a small carrier stored his vehicles. 'You
only have to depart a little from the daily routine to notice
that people are ingenious and manage to earn money,' he

thought. He had written his name on a page in a note-book. He was waiting. From time to time his face twitched. It was as if he was trying to chase away a fly walking about near his eyes, without using his hand. As a matter of fact it was not a real tic. Lesca could have got rid of it if he had wanted to, just as he could all the tics in his nostrils, lips and shoulders. There was a narrow bench between two windows. Lesca went up to the railing and, leaning over and speaking in a low voice, in a confidential tone, as if he was afraid of being heard by other people, he asked a clerk if he might be allowed to take the liberty of sitting down while he waited until the notary should do him the honour of agreeing to see him. The clerk looked at Lesca, wondering if he was making fun of him. The client's appearance must have reassured him, for he indicated by a slight protective gesture that he might sit down. Lesca thanked him several times, bowing as he did so. He might be kept waiting for a long time and he would quite understand, as he was not an important client, etc. He sat at the very end of the bench, put his hat on his knees and, looking straight ahead of him, he did not stir again.

'You can go in,' said the clerk after a few minutes.

Lesca did not reply. He pretended not to believe that he was being addressed already.

'Hey, you over there, sir, they're waiting for you.'

Lesca leapt up, assumed a distracted expression, and, as if he had lost his composure when faced with the great honour that was being done him, hurried towards the way out instead of going towards the door of Maître Donguy's office.

'You've got the wrong door,' cried the clerk.

Lesca stopped short. He looked all round beseechingly. 'Quick, quick,' he seemed to be saying, 'someone show me the way so I don't keep the great man waiting.'

'It's that door,' said the clerk again.

Everyone was laughing. Lesca, who had been bowing his thanks, went and knocked at the door.

'Come in,' cried a sharp voice from inside.

'Well, go in then,' said the clerks, seeing him remain motionless.

As soon as he had opened the door, even before he had taken a step, Lesca literally bent in half. The notary, astonished, stood up. Lesca went forward swinging his hat ceremoniously, as if he was performing a grand salute with every swing.

'I am extremely sorry, sir, to disturb you. I know that even the shortest time is valuable to a man like you. I shall only stay a few minutes.'

The notary was a worn, dried-up little man. A few grey hairs of different shades glued to his skull, not only wrinkles, but also small parts of his face which seemed dead, completely shrivelled, perfect false teeth with no shine, a fine great ring on his little finger, those were the details which made an immediate impression. For some minutes the noise of a starter motor had been rising from the courtyard. The car would not start. Every time the notary made a gesture of annoyance.

'Please, do sit down, sir,' he said, indicating one of the two leather armchairs opposite his desk where a husband and wife would usually sit.

Lesca sat on the edge of one of the chairs and, when he spoke, leaned forwards as if he wanted to be as close as possible to the notary and was frightened to speak out loud.

'I am a friend of one of your clients, Madame Maze,' murmured Lesca.

'You can speak up,' said Maître Donguy, 'nobody can hear you.'

'Oh! Thank you, sir. When I said "a friend" perhaps I was doing myself too much honour,' went on Lesca, turning round to see where he could tug at the armchair in order to get closer, but it was a massive piece of furniture rounded on all sides, and nothing jutted out. 'Madame Maze asked me, so to speak, to make an approach to you. Or, to be more precise, she did not ask me. She agreed that I should do it. But allow me to introduce myself. I can see that you are looking at the piece of paper on which I took the liberty of writing my name. I don't suppose it means anything to you. I am by way of being a local doctor. I am not even that now for I haven't practised for more than thirty years. I have been ill. I live for friendship above all. I have known Madame Maze for years. That's why you see me before you, sir. I told you that Madame Maze approved of the approach I am now making to you. You have only had a professional relationship with her, sir. I apologize again for

69

wasting your time, but in order to understand the meaning of my approach, it is necessary for you to be acquainted with all the little details I am laying before you. Madame Maze is a woman of immense qualities who has one fault, a fault which, I hasten to add, may not perhaps be one in your eyes. She is unhealthily proud. As you have been dealing with her affairs, you will remember, if indeed you can remember one particular and not very important case in the middle of all the weighty business in which you are concerned, you will remember that she left her husband – a man of feeling, it's true, but a devil for women – whom she married with a division of property settlement, and indeed I think it was you yourself who drew up the contract. So she left him, about fifteen years ago, and, with a pride to which I pay homage even though I cannot approve it, she preferred to leave behind everything that belonged to her rather than to have any dealings with her husband, even through intermediaries.'

Lesca broke off. 'A devil for women, division of property, the contract, homage,' he murmured. 'Grotesque. How shameful!' His eye began to quiver.

'It's not for me to judge the husband, sir,' went on Lesca. 'I don't know him. I don't expect to know him. But I think you will be of my opinion. In such circumstances, you would have acted as I did, you wouldn't have waited to be asked, you would yourself have seen to it that everything that belonged to this woman was returned to her. It was the natural action of a gallant man.'

Lesca broke off again. 'How shameful! How shameful! How could I have fallen so low?'

'He didn't do anything about it,' went on Lesca. 'I repeat, it's not for me to judge him. As is natural, Madame Maze tries to excuse him. She makes out that it's just forgetfulness on his part. I think so too. He is well off. Madame Maze's property could not fail to seem insignificant to him. When the property is reclaimed from him, he will be the first to be astonished at his conduct. Now, sir, be so good as to listen carefully. I shall soon be asking you what you think about the way I have acted. This is what I did. I told Madame Maze she was wrong. She is not rich. She works for a living. At last I persuaded her to reclaim her property. That is what I did. Did I do well? I am very uneasy at being here before you. My position is a delicate one.'

Lesca took out his handkerchief and rubbed his lip on which a kind of soft crust had formed. 'How shameful! How absurd!'

'I am embarrassed, sir,' he continued, 'at making you – oh! I'm sorry, the word just slipped out – I am embarrassed at putting you under the obligation of considering a particular case which is of so little interest. Did I do wrong? In fact, it's all one to me. Like you, I find that the conduct of Madame Maze is not without a certain nobility. As for me, her old friend, I am making use of my influence to bring the lady a little closer to reality. There's nothing very fine about that, is there?'

The notary smoothed his eyebrows with the tips of his fingers.

'I consider what you did entirely natural,' he said in a dry tone.

'Oh! thank you.'

'Don't thank me. You asked for my opinion and I gave it to you. That's all. Now I have to ask you a question in my turn. Did you come to see me in order to ask me what I thought about this matter or in order to ask me to put the situation right?'

'To ask you, if you agreed, of course, to put it right.'

'Very well. In that case I have to tell you at once that I can do absolutely nothing without a word from Madame Maze herself.'

Lesca reddened. In spite of that, he wanted to say something. But he could hear each word as if it was being uttered by someone else. He lost the thread of his thought. He stammered a few incoherent words.

'I am quite of your opinion,' said the notary, pretending not to notice anything.

'Of course, of course,' said Lesca at last. 'I was about to tell you that Madame Maze will be coming to see you.'

'There's no need for her to give herself that trouble.'

'Yes, yes, I know. Besides, my own role, my humble role is over. I have done all I could, as I always have done in my life. I couldn't have done more, could I?'

'A letter will be enough,' said Maître Donguy.

'You are too kind, sir.'

'As soon as I hear from her, I shall do what is necessary.'

Lesca stood up. He began bowing and scraping again. But he felt a kind of chill within him. He noticed that the notary merely pretended to show him out. He crossed the main room where the clerks were, gesturing towards the way out, so that it was clear he was leaving and would not be disturbing them much longer. On the wide stone staircase which was as draughty as the street and, like the street, lit by flickering gas-lamps, he stopped and straightened up. 'What an imbecile!' he said aloud. 'What a half-wit! Is it possible that there are such stupid people about!' He descended a few steps. 'And I'm an imbecile too.' Once outside, he went into the first café and had a stiff drink. 'It's always the same. Always the same difficulties, the same nasty tricks. Nothing works out as one wants or foresees. I ought to have said: I have come on behalf of Madame Maze. She requests you to do this and that. I was stupid. I was frightened. Frightened of what? Certainly not of him, but frightened of seeming like a crook, frightened he might say to himself: but what is there to prove that he knows my client? What is there to prove that she asked him to come and see me? And then I was ashamed too. I was ashamed of undertaking something like that. I've had enough of it, enough, enough. It's over. Gabrielle can do what she likes. I don't want anything more to do with that business. I say that every time. This time, it's the very last.'

When he reached home, he found Emily in the middle of writing to her son. On his way home he had thought some more about the visit to the notary. 'Perhaps he noticed that I was making fun of him. Perhaps I exaggerated. He suspected something. I didn't seem serious. Finally, in short, I made a mess of it, as usual.'

'Don't go on writing, Emily, please, it's not kind. Anyone would think I didn't exist as far as you were concerned.'

He spoke these words gently. He seemed like a man tempered by a great disappointment. He seemed to be saying: I now understand how badly I have treated you. She threw him a glance which showed he was disturbing her. She seemed to be saying: You might have had the decency to choose another time for your play-acting. The old muffler which unravelled if anyone tried to break off a loose piece of wool was round Lesca's neck. He had not taken it off. He sat down opposite his sister.

'Emily,' he said.

'What now?'

'I want to talk to you, Emily. I have something very important to say to you.'

'Yes, I know, always something very important.'

'Let me finish. But first I want you to make an effort to understand me. I am your brother . . .'

'Oh, heavens!' cried Emily.

'I'm not a stranger, I'm not an enemy. That's what you have to understand. If you understood, you would listen to me.'

'I am listening. You see, I've stopped writing.'

She adopted an attitude of resignation. He looked at her as a cripple might look at someone who was making fun of him, with an air of gentle reproach and faint menace. 'Ah, you're laughing! You're uncharitable. It's not right. But one day you'll be sorry. Then it will be too late.'

'Life separated us when we were young,' said Lesca bitterly. It has reunited us when we are old.'

Emily raised her head abruptly.

'Enough, I beg you. You don't believe a word of what you're saying. You're listening to yourself talking and I have to listen too. It's grotesque.'

He raised his eyes slowly, as people do who would like to have decided what to say before they met the glance of their companions.

'Come on, Emily,' he said at last.

'As soon as you begin talking like that, you know quite well you drive me mad. And you start again every time!'

'As soon as I begin talking like that? What? What do you mean? Like what? I talk, I always talk in the same way. I don't understand you.'

Emily's eyes glittered coldly.

'You understand me very well, Maurice. It's extraordinary. Why, I wonder, why can't you be natural? You're not sorry for anything. Nor am I. So, what?'

He did not reply. He rubbed his face with the flat of his hands, as if to wipe away the words in order to see things freshly. Then, with the apparent forgetfulness which kindly men make us believe in when they take offence at an impulse of anger, he said:

'When I am rich, Emily, there will be a great change, as if by chance. Then we shall understand each other. For I am going to be rich, Emily. Rich! the word is a bit strong. For I am going to have some money, a little money, Emily.'

'I'm very pleased for you.'

He seemed not to hear this ironic comment.

'Don't you want to know what I'm going to do when I have the money?' he asked.

'You'll do what you want . . .'

'My life will not change,' he went on, 'at least outwardly. I shall go and see Peix, as in the past. I shall prepare my own meals, as in the past . . . as in the past . . . It's not bad, is it? But I shall also do some extraordinary things.'

'Oh, good,' said Emily.

'Things you couldn't dream of.'

Lesca was becoming excited.

'You don't know me, Emily. Fate has kept us apart for too long. And when it reunited us, I was in a bad patch. How you see me today makes it impossible for you to get a picture of what I really am. You can't see a thing. You only see a tired old man, reduced to impotence. But just wait. When I have the money I'm talking about, you'll change your opinion of me, I assure you.'

'I hope you'll give me some,' said Emily, with an affected little laugh.

'Oh, no. Don't count on me. I shan't give you any money. One should never give money away.'

'I guessed as much,' she said with the same laugh. 'And I'm pleased to tell you that I shan't be asking for any.'

Lesca put his hat down on the table. All of a sudden he crushed it under his hand.

'Old rubbish,' he said, baring his teeth, 'second-hand old rubbish.'

'Here we go again.'

'You no more than anyone else,' Lesca went on. 'Nobody will touch a centime.'

Emily stood up.

'I would rather leave you,' she said.

'Fine, fine. Write to your son, your dear son. It's been such a long time, hasn't it, since you wrote to him?'

Emily turned.

'Don't talk about my son. Talk about whatever you like, but not about him.'

'He's a wretched idiot,' said Lesca.

Emily shrieked. For a moment she stood stock still, overcome with anger. She felt like striking her brother. But how? She began to tremble, then abruptly she ran into her own room.

At four o'clock, Lesca was with Madame Maze. Outside the sun was shining but in the windowless sitting-room the lamp was lit. The door was open. Daylight could be seen in the shop. Lesca was pacing to and fro, smoking a cigarette. 'It had to happen,' he said from time to time. Madame Maze was looking at him in astonishment but dared not ask him any questions.

'You hear me, Gabrielle, it had to happen. Little by little, without realizing it, I have put myself in your place. I understand now. I am getting mixed up in what does not concern me. It had to happen. I always want to be helpful, even when people are not anxious for it. And you are not anxious for it. But it's over. I won't have anything more to do with this business. You hear me, I won't have any more to do with it, any more to do with it. It's not pleasant to see people making fun of you. It's over.'

'That suits me very well,' said Madame Maze.

Lesca shrank back as if somebody had hit him.

'I thought,' he said, 'that at heart you wanted me to see to this business.'

'Well, I thought it was you who wanted to do it,' said Madame Maze.

'Me? Why me?' cried Lesca, going red.

'You kept on so. You kept on saying it was sensible and useful. I ended up believing you were right. What I know is that, left to myself, I wouldn't have done a thing.'

75

Lesca lit another cigarette.

'I don't know,' he said, 'why I went to see that Donguy fellow. I didn't want to go there, you understand, Gabrielle. I was aware it was ridiculous. And then I went. I said to myself: it's for her. But you didn't even want me to, Gabrielle. Put yourself in my place. What do I look like? I was wondering that this morning.'

Lesca broke off. He closed his eyes for a moment, then opened them again. He was weary.

'Actually,' he said after this silence, 'all this isn't very important.'

'You're right,' said Madame Maze.

Lesca felt a sinking sensation in the pit of his stomach. Immediately afterwards he smiled.

'I don't know, I shall never know how to show what I really am, shall I, Gabrielle?'

'Why?'

'It seems to me that, going by what I say, you can't fail to form a very strange opinion of me.'

'Not at all,' answered Madame Maze.

'You must imagine that I'm a very obstinate man, with only one object in mind, who only takes into account his own interests or the interests of people he cares for. His one aim in life is to win his case. The expression is exactly right. Win his case. In short, I'm a small man, petty and narrow, I am short-sighted. I can't see far ahead. I'm not in control of things. I'm well aware of it. That's what people must think of me.'

'Well, that's not the case with me,' said Madame Maze. 'I think quite the opposite.'

'You say that out of kindness, Gabrielle. Thank you. But I know perfectly well that I am nothing, neither what I said to you nor the opposite. Or rather, I do know what I am: a man who is obsessed with one thing, acting a part, who does not know how to do it. Anyway, all this isn't very interesting. What I am really has no importance at all.'

He bowed his head, then raised it again at once with a smile.

'You are in low spirits today,' said Madame Maze.

76

'Me! In low spirits! I'm never in low spirits. I don't know what low spirits are. I am perhaps – temporarily somewhat dejected.'

'Because of me?' asked Madame Maze.

'No. Because of everything. What I do leads nowhere, even when I succeed.'

'Come on, tell me, Maurice. What's happened? You seem so different today.'

'What's happened,' replied Lesca, 'is that this morning I came to understand a lot of things. What is happening to me has happened a hundred times before. But before, I couldn't understand the meaning of it. Now I can see my life. Everything is becoming clear. I think I am in control of what is going on and yet it always surprises me. In these conditions, it's better to stay calm, isn't it?'

'You are going through a bad patch, Maurice.'

'Perhaps,' said Lesca.

He sat down, leaned back in the chair and gazed at the light on the ceiling.

'You take things too much to heart, Maurice.'

He looked at Madame Maze with a grateful wry smile. Then he held out his hand, begging for an affectionate touch across the space between them. Madame Maze stood up and took a few steps in order to take hold of the hand.

'What a pity,' he said, 'that it's so late.'

His expression changed suddenly. She became uneasy. He pulled his hand away.

'What's the matter?' asked Madame Maze.

'There's one thing I can't bear,' he cried. 'That's it. That's it.'

'What?' asked Madame Maze.

'I don't want to hurt you, Gabrielle. I made you get up. I disturbed you. You came. I can't bear it. I'm angry with myself. I stretched out my hand to you. You were sorry for me, weren't you? "He's unhappy." That's what you thought . . . of course.'

Madame Maze took Lesca's hand again. He tried to pull it free, then left it where it was. For a few moments Gabrielle and Lesca stayed like that, beside each other, without moving or speaking. Suddenly Lesca stood up.

'I'm going,' he said.

'You're not leaving in that state, Maurice, you shan't leave, Maurice, until everything is sorted out. Don't be angry with me. I know it's all my fault. I'm sure of it. I wasn't willing. Now that I am willing, and am sure I am, the consequence is that I must act. You mustn't go. I want to give you a letter.'

Lesca was filled with immense joy.

'A letter,' he said, as if he did not understand.

Madame Maze had left the room. Lesca felt his heart pounding. 'I don't agree,' he said aloud. 'I don't want any more to do with this business. Any more at all. It's enough. I've done too much already. I'm not accepting and shall not accept the letter. I've had enough, enough, enough.'

'Here you are,' said Madame Maze, coming back.

He took the letter, held it in his hand for a moment, then put it in his pocket.

'I don't know why I'm taking the letter,' he said. 'I don't agree, I don't agree.'

'Oh, please do,' said Madame Maze. 'You mustn't get into such a state, especially when we can arrange everything so easily.'

He was making gestures whose meaning was impossible to guess. Were they gestures of refusal? No, because he still had the letter. Of acceptance? Not that either. They were signs of confusion. Lesca no longer knew what to say or what to do. Madame Maze was speaking to him gently. At that moment, words had no meaning. Madame Maze was aware that she had pleased Lesca, even if he made out that the opposite was the case. She was happy. Lesca reflected that there were men who accepted what they did not agree with. He was like them. Was it weakness? He could not answer. He had not agreed, he had accepted, but Madame Maze was a woman.

Lesca woke up with a start. It was light. The light bored painfully into his eyes.

'Emily,' he called.

Nobody answered. He realized that he was lying fully dressed on his bed. He was still wearing his shoes. His feet were frozen. He stood up.

78

'What are you doing, Emily?'

He looked at the time. It was three o'clock in the morning. Then he remembered that he had got home very late, at eleven o'clock, perhaps, that until then he had lingered in a café. Then he had cooked his dinner. But suddenly he had decided to eat later. He had put out the gas and stretched out on his bed, intending to get up again a bit later on.

'Emily,' he called again.

As his sister still did not reply, he went into her room and put on the light. She woke up and, even before she had realized what was happening, pretended not to have been asleep. She was always ashamed of sleeping, as if sleep were an indulgence.

'What do you want?' she asked.

He turned and looked about him. Then, as if he had only just understood what had happened, he said:

'So it wasn't you who left the light on. It was me.'

'You should go to bed,' said Emily.

He began to walk about the room without uttering a word. From time to time he threw a glance at his sister. She was leaning back on her pillow and had adopted the attitude of someone who is no longer thinking of sleep.

'I fell asleep,' said Lesca. 'That's something that never happens to me. And I'm not sleepy any more.'

He walked about for a little longer, then he sat down at the foot of the divan.

'You know, Emily,' he said very slowly and very calmly, 'some very extraordinary things are happening at the moment.'

She felt no curiosity to try and find out what he meant. She had long given up asking him questions. She hoped in this way to make him understand how much he riled her by talking in riddles.

'Very extraordinary things,' he repeated.

He looked at his sister. She was wearing a dirty grey cardigan and had a scarf round her neck. From what could be seen of her above the sheets she looked as if she was fully dressed. It was only her untidy hair and a certain cleanliness of face that showed that she was in bed.

'Am I disturbing you, Emily?' asked Lesca gently.

'No, but I think it's time you were in bed,' she said.

'Oh, yes!' he said. 'It's very late.'

He smiled.

'So you want me to go?' he asked.

'Yes, go to bed.'

He stood up.

'Goodnight, Emily. Goodnight,' he said slowly.

'Goodnight.'

'Do you want me to put out the light or will you do it yourself?' he asked.

'I'll do it.'

He went out, walking slowly like someone who does not know what he is going to do. For ten minutes or so he walked up and down his room. 'I haven't had any dinner,' he thought, 'but it's not worth the trouble now.' From time to time he looked to see if Emily had put out her light.

'Yes, Emily, some most extraordinary things . . .'

There was no reply.

'Are you asleep?' he asked.

'No, I'm not asleep.'

'It's pleasant, don't you think' Lesca went on, 'to be like everyone else?'

He stopped walking. Emily did not answer. He waited for a moment, then undressed slowly. Doing such simple things pleased him enormously. He got into bed and put out the light. Propping his head up against the wall, he looked at the light coming from Emily's room. He looked at it for a long time. Suddenly she extinguished it. He felt his chest contract. He almost asked Emily to put it on again. He did not dare. However he called:

'Emily!'

Not a sound broke the silence. He stretched out right to the end of his bed. The future seemed gloomy to him and full of danger, though there was nothing particularly threatening. And he managed to fall asleep.

One morning, as he was going to do his shopping, Lesca saw his name on an envelope which had been slipped between the curtain and the glass. He was seized with anxiety. He had recognized the writing of Madame Maze. He had been to see her every day except the previous one. What could have happened in so short a time? Sometimes he let three or four days go by without going to the bookshop and Madame Maze did not write to him. She knew he would always come in the end. Something unexpected must have arisen. He thought about the steps he had taken during the preceding fortnight. He had not concealed anything from Gabrielle. He tore open the envelope. Madame Maze begged him to visit the rue Monge that very day without fail. She had something very important to communicate to him.

Lesca walked as far as the place du Châtelet without seeing anyone. 'Nothing is following its usual course. A certain matter is over, or at least it seems so, and then some unforeseen event sets everything going again.' From time to time Lesca screwed up his right eye. 'What I'm doing is half-witted, half-witted, half-witted,' he said aloud. 'Wanting to get mixed up in something which is none of my business. It must be Donguy's doing. What a wretched fellow! Perhaps he imagines I am a u surper. He's criticizing me behind my back. He would like to say to me: "Oh, I'm so sorry, but Madame Maze didn't tell me the same thing".' Lesca stopped in order to cross a road. He was paying so little attention to what he was doing that several times he let the flood of vehicles set off again. 'So he was play-acting when he received me so politely.' Lesca crossed the road at last. 'How complicated life is! What is Madame Maze going to think? It's a waste of time bothering to make things simple and natural if an idiot like Donguy takes pleasure in knocking everything to the ground.'

Lesca retraced his steps, then went home. His fits of anger always finished like that. His first impulse was to get away, to go somewhere or other, then, as he grew calmer the further he went, he ended up by coming back again. As he climbed the stairs, though he tried to walk softly, the dog heard him and began to whine.

At four o'clock he went out again to see Madame Maze. He had been thinking. He had done his utmost to get outside himself, to sit in judgment on his way of behaving, to look at it with the eyes of an outsider. Of course some people (Donguy for example) might well consider he was playing a pretty wretched part. What kind of object was this unfortunate who had come down in the world, who had no means of support and was taking so much trouble about the money of a woman on her own? He lived with a sister whom he did not love and who, moreover, seemed not to have many illusions about him. He had taken advantage of the vague aspirations of one of those countless women for whom marriage had not been a success. He had played the part of the faithful friend. 'You ought to get back your money, believe me.' It was, needless to say, out of deep and sincere affection that he pressed the point like that, and not, as some people basely insinuated, with the ulterior consideration that there would always be a way of getting hold of the money!

Lesca slackened his pace. As that was how things were, there was only one way of getting out of the business, to tell Gabrielle what he had already told her so many times: I won't have anything more to do with this business. He straightened up. His part was over. He raised his head and looked at the first sticky, tightly folded buds growing miraculously from branches that were black, wet and dead. He had not been so happy for weeks. Nothing in his life was making him miserable any more. He was no longer saying to himself: I must say this or say that. He smiled at people. He apologized profusely whenever he got in anyone's way. 'It's unthinkable for me to annoy a passer-by at the moment!'

Before he went into the bookshop, Lesca had a look through the window. He was rather bashful, when there were customers there, about going through the shop and into the flat. With some difficulty – as Madame Maze, who did not care to be seen from the street, covered the glass door with magazines – he made out a woman and a small boy. The customer was hesitating over which note-book to choose. She picked up first one, then another. Madame Maze was watching her without interest. She did not know that Lesca could see her. Her manner was one he knew well, remote, as if she could not take her customers at all seriously or bring herself to give them any assistance. 'You ought to know what you want,' she seemed to be saying. A shopkeeper of whom people say: she's not really very pleasant. Lesca began to stroll about. Suddenly, catching sight of the shop from a distance, he was aware of a strange sensation. That shop there, in some street or other, was just like any other shop. There was nothing to draw the attention. And yet he knew everything that went on there. He was welcomed there as if it were his own home. He was familiar with all the idiosyncrasies of its owner. He had just seen her. At that very moment she was selling a note-book and no one was paying the slightest attention. There were thousands of similar shops in Paris, cleaners, hatters, dairies. As he passed by, he glanced covertly at the wretched displays where books of no interest got their value from paper-knives and leather articles. That shop was by no means unfamiliar to him.

At last the customer came out. Lesca did not go in straight away. He had just forgotten everything he had been preparing for hours beforehand. He closed his eyes for a moment. What he had to say came back to him.

'You wrote to me,' he said to Madame Maze as soon as she had joined him in the small windowless sitting-room. 'Why did you write to me? I don't understand. Anyone would think that I was involved in an affair of the utmost importance on your behalf. I am involved in absolutely nothing, as you well know, Gabrielle. There is nothing urgent, nothing serious. It's ridiculous. And that word: communicate. You have something to communicate to me. You can't have anything to communicate to me.'

Lesca pretended to laugh, but without conviction, simply going: ha, ha, ha!

'You don't know what has happened,' said Madame Maze.

'I tell you nothing can have happened, absolutely nothing, seeing that there is nothing.'

'Listen to me first. I've a letter from my husband.'

'You've never had a letter from your husband,' cried Lesca.

'Listen to me, please, Maurice. My husband is embarrassed. He is embarrassed. He has never given a thought to the question of interest. He is extremely sorry. Do you understand now? I'm in an appalling situation. What can he think of me? He had forgotten and I had not . . . No, Maurice, I should never have . . .'

Lesca was not drinking. Nevertheless his throat contracted several times in succession, as if he were swallowing mouthfuls of liquid one after another.

'Why?' he asked.

'Come on! Don't you understand? Yes, you do. You know quite well that certain things remain between a man and woman who have loved each other which must not be touched. One cannot touch them.'

'Right! I've had enough,' said Lesca, suddenly no longer knowing what he was saying. 'Obviously there are things which mustn't be touched, which can't be touched. I can't touch them either. I don't know why you mentioned them. They are nothing to do with me. The love of others is nothing to do with me. Well, I've had enough, quite enough. Long ago. I tell you so every time. It's you who don't listen to me. Why a letter, I mean your letter? There's no need for a letter. It's pointless. I tell you again, I've had enough.'

'Don't be angry with me, Maurice.'

'Me! Angry with you? Whatever for? This whole business leaves me quite cold.'

'I beg you, Maurice, don't be angry with me. I assure you my behaviour is quite natural and no woman of feeling would reproach me. I don't want to ask for anything back from my husband, anything at all. I don't need anything. Explain that to Donguy. He is to write to my husband and say he made a mistake. And you, don't be angry.'

Lesca put a hand to his throat, as if to help the contraction. His lips were compressed. A hollow had formed at each side of his nostrils.

'Donguy, Donguy!' he cried. 'Me explain something to Donguy! But I despise Donguy. He's the type of person I simply can't stand. And why do you keep on telling me not to be angry with you?'

'I feel I am hurting you, aren't I, Maurice?'

'Hurting me? Why, why? There are times when I can't make you out, Gabrielle. Do whatever you like. You are free. I am only a friend. Do everything you want. I have no advice to give you. I don't know why I should have got mixed up in this business. I have no interest in it. I wonder every time. It's for your good, perhaps. I really don't know. Do what you

84

want. If it bothers you, if it's too much for you, well, don't do it. It's quite simple. It all seems quite simple to me. I don't know why we keep talking about it all the time.'

'Forgive me, Maurice. I made a mistake. I thought I could bear anything, and you see, at the first blow, I can't. Promise not to hold it against me.'

Lesca stood up abruptly.

'You don't know what you are saying, Gabrielle.'

Even before she could reply, he was gone. Looking neither left nor right, he crossed the street. He was walking as quickly as he could. Then he crossed the street again. He dimly wanted not to be knocked down but to be brushed by a car. A driver swore at him. He turned round, gesticulated wildly and set off straight ahead. So he had behaved in such a way that Madame Maze, as soon as she gave something up, was convinced that she was hurting him. Ten times in succession he had told her that she was not hurting him at all and was free to do what she wanted, but she did not believe him. The more he denied it, the more she was convinced that he was in pain and begged him to forgive her. What had he done? What could she read in his face? Would she never understand that he did not take this business seriously, that the only reason why he had kept on about it and embarked on certain undertakings was a kind of pity. He could not tell her that. But it was the truth. He often pitied her. He had again just recently, when he had seen her through the window, so sad, so remote, beside that woman who was choosing a note-book. He was fond of Madame Maze. He wanted to make her life more pleasant, to shield her from difficulties if anything should happen to her or if she should fall ill. He knew what it was. The professor had saved his life. He knew what it was to be obliged to feel gratitude, and people are condemned to feel it at times when they have failed to make provision. And instead of understanding all this, Gabrielle imagined that she was hurting him.

He retraced his steps. He was calmer. In leaving as he had, impulsively, he was well aware that he was providing Madame Maze with yet another reason for thinking she had hurt him. 'He was so terribly angry to learn that I didn't want to ask anything of my husband that he went off like a madman.' He must put things straight.

'Gabrielle,' he said, as soon as he was back, 'I have returned as you see. I have decided, as you know, not to have any more to do with your business. But there must be no misunderstanding. I went off just now in a way that must have surprised you. You doubtless thought the cause of it was your change of attitude. Well, it wasn't. I have no reason at all to lose my temper when you decide on one thing rather than another. I tell you once more: you are free. It's not that. I went away because you seemed to be afraid of hurting me. Come, Gabrielle! How can you hurt me? I put the question to you. It's impossible. You cannot hurt me, any more than you will give me any pleasure. The money belongs to you. Take it or not, do what you want. But I beg you, don't go and think that if you don't take it you will hurt me. I am astonished that you can't see that there is something wounding in that.'

Madame Maze was standing near the door, as women often do stand, with no special reason for being in a place.

'My poor Maurice,' she said after a few moments, interrupting him.

He looked at her in astonishment.

'My poor Maurice,' she repeated.

'You think I deserve pity?' he asked ironically.

'I'm a difficult woman, aren't I?'

'Why?'

'I'm such a nuisance to you!'

Lesca felt his right eye-lid begin to quiver. He stopped it with his finger. He was a big man. He was even more conscious of it because the air he drew in and exhaled made so much noise.

'Not in the least,' he replied drily.

'I'm wrong,' went on Madame Maze. 'I realize I'm wrong, Maurice. Just now, when you were away, I was thinking. Well, I have decided to change. The worst type of woman is the one who hangs on to extremely honourable feelings, worthy of respect, whose object is another man. You have to abandon everything when you love, don't you, Maurice?' Even what gives an exalted idea of our character. If you were not here, my behaviour would seem natural, noble, beautiful, anything you like. But you are here! Ah, well, I mustn't bore you any longer with my conceit, vanity and pride. Let's forget all that. Carry on, Maurice. Don't bother about me. Do what you wanted to do.'

Lesca grew red with happiness. His face was usually so drawn, his eye-lids so heavy and his complexion so ashen that when he reddened it seemed as if he had just made an enormous effort.

'It would be better not,' he said. 'We shall be happier if we don't talk about this business any more.'

Madame Maze smiled. She went up to Lesca and took his arm as if they were about to go out together.

'But we must get this business settled.'

'No,' said Lesca.

'Oh yes,' she went on, 'otherwise, I'm sure there will always be something not quite right.'

Lesca stammered out a few words. He no longer knew where he was. When he left his ears were burning. What sort of man was he in Gabrielle's eyes? 'What can she think of me?' he kept on wondering. 'I refuse . . . and then I agree. But why does he always agree? It's appalling. Heavens, how difficult it is to be oneself with some people!'

From his bed, Lesca was looking at the shutters. The metal slats were tilted in such a way as to shut out the light from the street. One of them was worn away like an old shovel. At this point alone the light could be seen. Lesca knew that the yellower the patch was, the darker it was outside. He had been asleep for scarcely an hour and already he had a bitter taste in his mouth. 'It's my liver,' he thought. He passed his hand over his face. He heard the noise made by his bristles, a noise he alone could hear, like the noise he made when he crunched a sugar lump. A slight pain, a bit like the pain cause by harmless neuritis, tightened his chest. He sat up, hoping it would disappear. He felt old and dirty, in the middle of his sagging bed, covered with worn-out clothes, in the sheets where his feet and head had left grimy marks. He could smell flannel hard with dried sweat under his arms, he could smell his over-heated feet, damp in the socks which he kept on when he went to bed and was not brave enough to take off afterwards. But the yellow patch was growing paler, gold was turning to primrose. Day was dawning. He got out of bed and got dressed immediately, putting on his collar, his tie and even his hat. Then he felt better. He always dressed like that, at night, when he got up. He had a foreboding that he would die in his bed, in the middle of a tangle of clothing, all covered in sweat, trembling with fever, powerless to move. And every time he was on his feet, with his hat on his head, he felt he was no longer afraid of anything. It was half past three. He walked about for an hour, noiselessly, as he did on the second-floor landing. Among all the clothes on his bed there was one real bedcover. He sat in the armchair, wrapped up his legs and, still wearing his hat, stayed sitting there, with the light on. Suddenly the cheerful noise of the milk-cart and the churns being banged down on the pavements roused him from his torpor. It was six o'clock in the morning. The night had ended some time before, more than an hour before, at the time when the cart had left the depot, at half-past four or five o'clock. Lesca used to think about that cart when he could not sleep. It comforted him to know it was on its way.

Lesca dropped off to sleep several times. When it was completely light, he went into the kitchen and drank a cup of coffee. Then he walked round his room for about twenty minutes. 'I shall go today. I must go. Then I shall be rid of it, as they have been waiting for me for three days. I shall end up by falling ill.' He went out. Nothing that made up spring could yet be seen, flowers, fruit, or leaves on the trees, not even sunshine, but the softness of springtime could be felt beneath the coolness of the air. Lesca walked along the noisy streets, under the light grey sky, with the delight of a convalescent. However, at certain moments, his face wore a mournful expression. He went along the rue de Rivoli as far as the Hôtel de Ville. Then he retraced his steps and went up the boulevard Sébastopol. He looked at all the clocks. Time was not moving forward. Sometimes he even went back a bit when, as he looked at the time, his eyes fell on a clock that was slow. 'I must wait until ten o'clock,' he said from time to time. 'It's a form of torture not to be able to do immediately something that has been decided after much hesitation. I'd have done better to be hesitating still or at least to have waited to decide what I should do.'

Where the wide boulevards crossed, he turned left. It had been ten to ten a while before. It could not still be ten to ten. It must be ten o'clock. In the boulevard Bonne-Nouvelle, he stopped in front of Donguy's building. Before he went in, he looked round anxiously. He made sure that nobody had stopped and, although he could not have said why, he felt relieved. He went under the archway and up the two flights of stairs. In the office there was that atmosphere peculiar to working days that are just beginning. Nothing unexpected could happen and yet there was something cheerful about it. Like a suspect looking for a document, Lesca showed a letter to a clerk.

'Please wait, sir,' came the answer.

He stationed himself in front of a window, facing the courtyard. He was trembling slightly. 'It's not for me, it's not for me,' he kept saying under his breath. 'I shouldn't be trembling like this.' His mouth was half open. He tried to close it, but then he could not breathe.

'You can come, sir,' said the clerk after a few minutes, lifting up a section of the railing.

Lesca pretended not to understand. The clerk had to tell him again that he could come. Then, as if he had been invited to enter some holy place, Lesca took off his overcoat, hastened to lay it down on the bench, smoothed his hair with his hand, tightened his tie, pulled down his jacket, then, apologizing, constantly enquiring if he might come forward, he went and sat down at the clerk's small table. The clerk opened a cigar box in which were some girlish trinkets. He had a pencil in his hand. In front of him was a typed list. At his feet Lesca noticed two bundles wrapped in newspaper and tied up roughly with string.

'Have you got your list, sir?' asked the clerk.

'No, no,' stammered Lesca, 'but it doesn't matter, it's not important. I'll refer to yours.'

When the checking of the jewellery was finished, the clerk untied the bundles. One of them contained a fur coat, the other some sheets and a small statue.

'It's pathetic,' said Lesca.

The clerk looked up in astonishment.

'No, no, I was thinking about something else,' said Lesca.

The door of the office closed by itself. Lesca had opened it with the help of his feet. He held a bundle in each hand. He was thinking: 'What an idea to get mixed up in this affair! And these people, what wretched people!' The sun was about to break through. It could be seen, as yet without definite shape, in the grey sky. Lesca crossed the boulevard and took a little street which led towards the centre. He no longer knew where he was going. His only thought was to get away and lose himself. The pavements were narrow. In that commercial district he was not the only one carrying parcels, and this comforted him. 'At last Gabrielle will be pleased,' he thought, 'because it's hers.' Then he recalled the checking ceremony. 'How shaming!' Lesca himself had taken part in the checking. It had seemed to him that one of the trinkets was missing. He had pointed it out because he had Madame Maze's interests so much at heart. 'We'll find it,' the clerk had said. 'It must be here somewhere.' The trinket had indeed been found. 'How shaming!' Lesca had thanked him when he left. There is something ambiguous in the thanks people utter when they are taking money away. Had he been saying thank you for the trouble he had caused or for the money itself? The fur coat had had to be tied up again. The clerk had apologized for wrapping the parcels so badly. Lesca had had to help him. They had had to ask another clerk for some string. Nobody had had any. And then Donguy had appeared to give the money to the clerk and he had a receipt in his hand to which he plainly attached as much importance as to the money. Lesca had risen to his feet, but the notary had seemed not to recognize him. 'Incredible, absolutely incredible!' Yet he had seen him clearly. Without a doubt he had come to make sure that Lesca really was Lesca. How despicable it had all been!

Lesca went into a café, sat down and put the parcels on the bench near him. There was a clock facing him. He was astonished to see that it was a quarter past twelve. Two hours, that comedy had gone on for two hours. He ordered a sandwich and ate a hard-boiled egg while he was waiting for it. His eyes were lowered. He was not saying anything, but his lips kept on separating slightly and then closing again in a steady rhythm. All of a sudden he stood up, paid and went out. The sun was out at last, but too late. It was the sun of any ordinary afternoon. Lesca caught a bus. From his place he could see the crowd he was leaving behind, continually received. He could see a cyclist. He could see the conductor's strange little machine. 'That's very French,' he thought. Suddenly he remembered the cigar-box. He had forgotten it. Supposing somebody had stolen it? 'That would be the last straw', he said aloud. His neighbour turned towards him. Lesca bowed his head.

As soon as he was at home, he locked the door behind him. Emily was in the kitchen. She never did a thing there. When her brother asked her to come, she always replied: in a moment. She said to Lesca:

'Have you had your lunch?'

'Yes,' he answered.

The newspapers wrapping up the fur coat had been cut through by the string. Lesca did up the parcel again, then he went and put it in the corner between the head of his bed and the sideboard, behind the chair he used as a bedside table. Just then Emily came into the room. He sat down in the leather armchair. In the early afternoon the sun, passing between two houses, shone into the flat for half an hour. Lesca lit a cigarette. He put it to his lips and inhaled the smoke deeply, then his whole body was shaken by a strange movement. It was as if, just for a moment, the touch of his clothing had become intolerable to him. He threw away his cigarette. The corners of his mouth were drawn back. He seemed to be in pain. Nevertheless, a few moments later, he began to hum a tune, beating time imperceptibly. But he very soon stopped. He was still short of breath from the morning's efforts. He rose to his feet and walked up and down the room. Every time he passed the cigarette he had just thrown away, he ground it down again. Emily was doing her washing-up. He sat on his bed and glanced at the fur coat.

'Emily,' he cried suddenly, so loudly that Emily came out of the kitchen at once.

He had fallen on to his side. With one hand he was tugging at his tie, making it tighter instead of undoing it. His other hand was waving about above his head. He was stamping on his own feet, as if a more severe pain might drive away a lesser one. His eyes could not be seen because they were squashed between the arch of his brows and his cheeks. Emily, without apparent emotion, looked about her for some means of relieving him. She had made no move when Lesca straightened up. He looked at Emily   with no sign of recognition. He was breathing very quickly.

'I thought I was going to have a seizure,' he said.

She helped him to lie flat.

'The truth is there was nothing the matter with you,' she said.

'I was frightened. I managed to forestall it. It's quite instinctive.'

She shrugged her shoulders.

'I'll bring you a cup of coffee,' she said.

When she returned, his eyes were closed, his hands folded over his stomach. He was breathing calmly, in a strange way. Every time he breathed out, he formed his lips into a round, so that he looked as if he was blowing on something. As soon as Emily went away, he raised his eye-lids, revealing two pale eyes. When Emily came back, he did not close them.

'I thought you were asleep,' she said. 'Do you want your coffee?'

He did not answer. His mouth was no longer round. It remained half open.

'Maurice,' she cried, suddenly afraid.

He turned his head slowly towards her.

'What's the matter with you?' asked Emily.

'I'm getting better.'

Lesca had not stirred when night fell. The lights from the street danced on the ceiling. There was a light on in Emily's room.

'Emily,' he called.

'Yes,' she said.

'What time is it?'

'Eight o'clock.'

He got up and briefly smoothed his bed. He was feeling much better. He dampened his hair and made himself look a bit fresher. Then he dawdled about for a while. When people have been in bed for a long time, they like to assure themselves of their freedom of movement by touching everything.

92

'I'm going for a little walk,' he said to his sister.

There were still a great many people in the streets, for it had been a fine day. Some cafés had opened their glass screens. The air was extraordinarily clear. Lesca went towards the place du Châtelet. He did not often go out in the evening. He sometimes came back late, but almost never went out once he was at home. He crossed both branches of the Seine. He was going to the rue Monge, though he had not decided to do so, letting himself be carried along, as if he were seeing some friends home in a district which for the time being had no interest for him. But when he found himself in the immediate vicinity of the bookshop, his heart began to pound. His poor heart, he really had overworked it in the course of his life. Impossible to give it any rest. Again today, and despite all his precautions, Lesca could not organize his life in such a way as to leave it in peace. Nevertheless, in settling in the rue de Rivoli, he had done what he could. Why should he now be surprised at all the troubles he was experiencing? He caught sight of Madame Maze's narrow shop, unlit like all the others, but so modest that she had no need of a metal shutter to protect it. A gas-light outside it lit up the sleeping window-display. Lesca stopped to see if a light was shining through a half-open doorway. There was nothing. Madame Maze was shut up in her rooms. Unless she was out. He retraced his steps. His heart was beating just as hard, though without any real cause, all by itself, like an organ which has just made a tremendous effort. Lights were trembling on the water, like twisted sword-blades. The time when he used to roam the night with his friends was long gone. But nothing had changed. Policemen still wore capes and beggars still pushed their hands into their sleeves.

There was a light on in Emily's room. He went in. Emily was doing her knitting, her eyes on the tips of her needles, but her thoughts were elsewhere. Lesca sat down on the only chair in the room. He stayed like that for almost an hour, without saying a word, lighting cigarette after cigarette. Eventually, annoyed by this presence, Emily said she was going to put out the light. He looked at her for some time, without saying a word. She knew he liked arousing curiosity by keeping silent.

'What's the matter?' she asked, irritated.

He went on staring at her.

93

'Leave me,' she said.

'Nothing's the matter,' he replied at last.

'After what happened to you,' Emily went on, 'you would do better to rest than to indulge in play-acting.'

'So you don't understand?' asked Lesca.

'No.'

He stood up, made as if to leave, then came back to his sister. His gloomy and mysterious expression had gone. He looked at her affectionately. He gave her his hand.

'Goodnight,' he said.

He went out slowly. At the door he turned.

'Think,' he said.

She had put down her work. She raised her head, revealing her bare neck.

'What do you want me to think about?'

'Your future. I may not always be here. People may not always give me money. I could die.'

He had hardly finished speaking when she put out the light.

'You're wrong,' he said, without moving in spite of the darkness.

He heard an 'oh' of weariness.

'Remember what I am saying. It will soon be too late.'

She put the light on again.

'What do you mean? Why too late?'

'Don't be cross, Emily. It's for your good that I'm talking like this. Look at how you live. You aren't happy. I can't make it any clearer.'

'Am I a nuisance to you?'

'No. You aren't a nuisance. You'll never be a nuisance. But you are younger than I am. You are in better health. And you have a son, whom you love. You could live in your own house, independent and happy . . . if you wake up . . . you understand. You must wake up. You are too forgetful of reality.'

Emily tried to read the meaning of these words on her brother's face. But an expression of great kindliness concealed his true feelings.

'Please don't talk about my son,' she said.

'Think, Emily. I'm only thinking of your good.'

'Thank you,' she replied drily.

94

He went away, then, changing his mind, came back to his sister once more.

'You are intelligent enough to understand me, Emily. You ought to go out and see people. If you stay shut up here, nobody will ever take any interest in you. If you go out, perhaps some sort of opportunity will arise, who knows?'

'What sort of opportunity?' cried Emily. 'Honestly, there are times when I wonder if you aren't mad. You have such a strange way of seeing things . . .'

'A chance I mean. You know better than I what you want. I suppose that, like everyone else, you would be happy to have some money. Why don't you ask people who have money to give you some? They might be very glad to do so.'

Emily shook back her sparse hair like a young woman. She looked at her brother challengingly, in a peculiarly feminine way.

'Do you really want me to ask you, you, for money?'

'Ask me?' cried Lesca, leaving his mouth open to show how astounded he was.

'Oh, stop play-acting!'

'Play-acting?'

'You're right,' said Emily. 'Your affairs are nothing to do with me. They are of no interest to me. And I don't want to know anything about them.'

'I, give you money!' went on Lesca. 'But where, in heaven's name, would I get it from?'

'Oh, Maurice, have pity on me, give me something,' begged Emily ironically.

'Yes, if you wish,' said Lesca.

It was impossible to make out whether he was speaking seriously or not. Emily could not keep up the irony for long. Her face crumpled.

'Oh, no!' she said.

'Come on!' exclaimed Lesca gently.

'I'll never accept anything from you, you hear, never,' she cried.

'All right, all right,' said Lesca kindly, 'but if you aren't willing to accept, you can take.'

This observation surprised Emily so much that she was struck dumb.

'Take?' she enquired at last.

'Yes, take.'

'Steal, you mean.'

'Why not?'

'Honestly, it's impossible to talk to you,' she said. 'You sometimes go off your head. Steal. You talk about it quite coolly, as if it was entirely natural. Do you really know what you are saying?'

'I never told you to steal. You're the one who's mad.'

He took a few steps and turned to leave the room.

'I tell you again, you're wrong,' he said.

'That's enough,' said Emily, pulling up her covers and thumping her pillow as if she was on the point of going to sleep.

'Think,' said Lesca again.

Emily put out the light and did not reply. He had to make his way cautiously to the light-switch of his room. Then he closed his sister's door. For a while he remained motionless. 'How shameful,' he murmured, catching sight of the parcel at the head of his bed. 'Those scraps of gold, and those fragments of jade, and those stones without settings!'

On the afternoon of the following day he went out, intending to go and visit Professor Peix. 'The visit is obviously the right thing in the circumstances. I shall ask him for two hundred francs. The moment could not be more appropriate.' But as he went along he changed his mind. The prospect of a conversation with someone other than Emily made him dreadfully apprehensive. As he left home he had caught sight of the concierge under the archway. Simply in order to avoid greeting him, he had stayed on the staircase for several minutes, pretending to look for something in his briefcase. 'I ought to have suspected I wouldn't go to the professor's. Then I needn't have bothered with this journey,' he said as he reached the boulevard Raspail. He went to wander about in the Luxembourg. From time to time he stopped to watch the children playing. Some of the parents smiled at him. He spoke to them. Though he recoiled from speaking to people in his own circle, he very much enjoyed talking to strangers. They took pleasure in showing that they were sensible and reasonable. The generalities they exchanged were evidence of a humane and cheering desire to get along together. Lesca felt himself to be quite harmless. He was no longer an actor. The words that issued from his lips were true, honest and generous. He was filled with great confidence in himself. After all he was the good man who was smiled at by mothers of families. So was he doubtful about it? It was possible to have struggled throughout life without thereby becoming a man under suspicion. What had happened the day before was quite normal. He could well have been tired. Those mothers would have understood very well. Of course, he ought to have gone to the rue Monge the day before. But he had been unable to, and, when he had gone there, it had been too late. Besides, there was no hurry. Madame Maze had been waiting for ten years, twenty years, he did not know exactly. How could he suppose that she would be impatient at a delay of twenty-four or forty-eight hours, when two days before she had not even wanted to hear Donguy's name mentioned?

All of a sudden there came to him the idea of going to see her at once, without waiting a minute. He would bring her up to date with what had happened. He would laugh, talk of other things. That business was fundamentally unimportant. Madame Maze had said so often enough. Nevertheless he stayed and walked about in the Luxembourg for a while. He walked slowly. Every time he sat down, he found he could not stay still and got up at once. At last he set off towards the rue Monge. As soon as he found himself a hundred yards or so from the bookshop, he realized that he would not go in, that he would no more find the strength to speak to Madame Maze than he had to speak to the concierge a short while before. For a moment he even had the feeling that he would never be able to speak to anyone again. A look of deep anxiety appeared on his face. As sometimes happens, a passer-by gazed at him intently. He turned away his head. What had the passer-by been thinking? He saw himself, as it were from without, in that unattractive street, shabbily dressed, hunching his massive shoulders, his right foot turned involuntarily inwards, and his delicate weasel face, a child's face above a double chin, pitted so much that, even when he had just shaved, it still bore countless traces of blemishes, tears, cuts and chaps, and fragments of dry white skin on the lips. He had met men like that before, but had not paid any attention to them, men much older than he was, imprisoned in old age, so that it was impossible to tell whether they had been good or wicked. Today he had become like them. He gazed at the bookshop. A year earlier, when he had been courting Madame Maze, he had found himself very near the bookshop but in the same way quite unable to go in. He was jealous. He had kept watch on the door of the shop from a small café such as can be seen at the ends of empty streets with tiny tables and bars. He had sat next to the window and watched, like so many men with nothing to do.

He crossed the street, intending to pass in front of the bookshop. But Madame Maze often used to look out across the window display to amuse herself. He did not dare. He went into the little café and stayed standing. There was a light in the bookshop, although there was no need for it, as it was still daylight. Gabrielle was waiting for him. When he went every day, the shop was in darkness. If he missed one, that light was there waiting for him the next day. After an hour he went away. 'I shall come back,' he said.

When he reached home, he realized that his journey to the rue Monge had not been entirely useless. Because of it, he was returning home without fear. How confused he would have felt if he had not spent an hour very near Madame Maze! As soon as he had closed his door, he began to tremble. Emily was not there. Even though he told himself that she went down to fetch her milk every day at that time, he went on trembling. 'But what am I afraid of?' he wondered. The parcel was still at the head of his bed. He sat down so that he should make no noise and thus be able to catch the smallest sounds of coming and going. Suddenly the door opened. It was Emily. He let out a deep and noiseless sigh.

'Oh, you've been out!' he said.

'I've been to fetch the milk.'

'Why was I afraid?' he wondered again.

'Have you thought about it?'

'Are you starting that again?'

'I should like to know if you've thought about it.'

98

'About what?'

'You know very well. You are capable of doing something at the moment. But, in order to do it, you have to want to. It isn't difficult.'

'Would you like me to go back to Bordeaux?' asked Emily.

'Oh, no, certainly not. You would be unhappy down there. And what about your son? You wouldn't want to live far from him. You don't see him, but you know he's there. But at Bordeaux . . .'

'What then?'

'Because you love your son, because you love him . . . it seems to me that ought to give you courage, boldness . . .'

'Honestly, I don't understand you.'

All of a sudden, Lesca strained his ears.

'Do something,' he whispered, tip-toeing towards the main door.

'What's the matter?' asked Emily.

'Be quiet. Can't you hear somebody walking? I think someone's coming upstairs. Is someone coming up?'

'What does it matter?'

'It doesn't.'

He leaned against a wall. He ran his thumb several times over the ends of his fingers. And indeed it made a sound like footsteps, but the sound got no nearer.

'There's nobody coming up,' said Emily.

'So what is it?'

'A noise in one of the flats.'

Lesca came back to Emily.

'It's a noise of footsteps,' he said. 'You can hear it quite well, thump, thump. It's footsteps.'

Emily wondered what was the matter with her brother. She looked at him as if, in a dangerous situation, he had suddenly fallen ill.

'The noises must be coming from the studio on the third floor. You can hear that they are not coming nearer or going away.'

'That's true,' said Lesca, growing calmer. 'Even if they were getting nearer it wouldn't matter at all.'

There was a newspaper lying on a chair. He put it on the table and sat down. Emily had withdrawn to her own room.

'One thing annoys me,' he said after a while. 'You never understand what I say to you.'

'That's because there's nothing to understand,' she replied.

'But I'm speaking quite plainly. I'm telling you to do something.'

'Oh, don't start again.'

'Do something. You'll never find a better time.'

'You want me to go to Noyon.'

'No, no. You must be independent. You could be. It all depends on you. You only have to want to. You are incapable of wanting! There was no need for all that trouble with your son. You keep on saying that I'm play-acting. But you are. At heart you are glad not to see him any longer. Your sacrifices, you make too much of your sacrifices.'

Emily appeared in the doorway.

'Be quiet,' she said. 'If you go on, I shall write to Monsieur Peix.'

'To Peix! Well, write to him. That's fine by me. He'll tell you just the same. Something must be done, Emily. You must do something. You could do it now. So you don't understand. I can't do anything, but you should. You love someone, you love your son. It would be so easy. You only have to take what you find and go away if you want to live and be happy with your son near you. Then he will be full of admiration for you. That's what I should do, if, of course, I were in your place.'

Emily smiled at her brother. She glanced quickly at the door. She was frightened.

'What do you mean, I ought to take what I find?'

'You do something. You take action.'

'So again I have to find something.'

'You can always find something if you really want to.'

This time Emily could not restrain herself.

'I didn't think you were capable of speaking like that. I should have suspected it. I've known you long enough.'

She went into the kitchen, banging the door behind her.

At the same time Lesca went and hurled himself on to his bed.

'Emily,' he cried.

She did not even hear him.

'Ah, ah, ah, ah!'

He was all knotted up on himself. He was so big and heavy that he seemed incapable of simply getting up.

'I'm suffocating, I'm suffocating,' he cried again. 'Oh, heavens, what pain, what pain! Come here, Emily.'

Emily opened the door. She gave her brother a worried look. There were great drops of sweat on his forehead. They were not running down, so it was as if he had an illness in which the natural functions had ceased to work. Emily felt his pulse, then struggled to put him into a more comfortable position.

'What's the matter?'

'The door, the door,' he murmured.

She ran to the main door, then came back saying that there was nobody there. She had come to the conclusion that he was afraid someone was coming to see him. He had straightened up. He had wiped the centre of his forehead. Large drops of sweat remained untouched on his temples.

'Are you in pain, or not?' she asked him.

'I'm not in pain.'

'Then what is all this play-acting about?'

'It isn't play-acting,' said Lesca, forming the words with difficulty. 'You banged the door. I told you before. I thought I was going to have a seizure. I can't tolerate anything. The noise frightened me so much that I thought . . .'

He stood up and smoothed his hair.

'Did you get some milk for me?' he asked.

They both sat down at the table.

'Now you're calm,' said Emily, 'I'm going to ask you one thing. Why, for the past few days, have you been so concerned with me? You know perfectly well I shall never ask you for anything.'

Lesca slammed his hands down on the table so hard that it felt as if the tips of his fingers were being pierced by needles.

'That's all it needed,' he yelled.

Emily jumped up and ran into her room. But she did not bang the door.

Once he was in bed, Lesca found he could not sleep. He was over-wrought. He was hot. He kept on lifting up the covers to cool himself, but never for long enough. Round about one in the morning, however, he began to grow calm. He no longer felt the need to keep moving. The heat gradually receded from his limbs and forehead. He felt it was entirely up to him whether he went to sleep. Although his eyes were closed and he sometimes had the troublesome sensation that they were open underneath his lids, his brain was functioning perfectly. He was thinking clearly and simply, as if he had just got up and it was daytime. He could hear Emily sleeping, her sleep divided into phases of about ten minutes. From the time when he began to feel well, he did not mind not sleeping nor being disturbed by the noise. On the contrary, he rather liked it. He was glad of the long breathing-space and when he heard the clocks striking in the distance the passing of time was as disagreeable to him as when he was at the theatre. He took care not to open his eyes, for fear of breaking the spell.

Although he usually woke up at four or five in the morning, he slept peacefully until eight o'clock. Emily was already up. She spent the mornings busily doing things which were the result of decisions she had made in bed and which, for the most part, were quite useless. Lesca did not speak to her at all. This often happened when he was not feeling well-disposed towards her. This time his thoughts were elsewhere and he did not even see her.

After lunch, Lesca began to get agitated again. He had not made his bed nor had he shaved. Each of these operations took him some minutes. He kept thinking about them but he could not make up his mind to do them. He walked rapidly round the small flat, then he sat down and wondered why he was sitting down. Finally he went out. In front of the house he stood still for a moment, puzzled. 'Why did I come out?' He watched the crowds passing by. They were not divided into two separate streams, one going up and the other down. They mingled ceaselessly but never came to a halt. He went in the direction of the rue Monge. It was absurd. He knew quite well he would not go in to see Madame Maze, but he could not do anything else. He needed to see the bookshop, even from a distance, to recover his peace of mind. While he was on the way he thought about himself again. He could not deny it, he was insignificant. He went into the little café. Only a little while before, when he went into a place frequented by labourers, he was convinced that people nudged one another and thought him a bit of an intruder because they reckoned he was of a different social class. That bothered him. Although he was very good at not appearing proud, he was afraid he might betray himself by some detail. But now, whether because customs had changed or because he had lost what distinguished him from less well-off people, nobody paid any attention to him. He caught sight of himself in a mirror. He certainly belonged to another class, but was so tired and worn out that he could no longer represent it.

He spent the afternoon watching the door of the shop. Whenever a woman pushed the door open, he was quite undisturbed. But when it was a man, especially if the man did not look too stupid, if he was dressed in a perfectly ordinary way, without affectation, neither shabbily nor ostentatiously, he would glue his forehead to the thin glass or even go out in front of the café, while his poor heart began to pound again.

The next morning, as he was passing by the lodge, the concierge handed him a letter. A rush of blood rose to his head. 'Ah, yes,' he said, taking the letter and instinctively concealing his discomfort. He had put it in his pocket as if it had been some sort of circular. He even went back to ask the concierge if there was anything else for him. He immediately turned down a narrow street, then down another, narrower still. He needed to be on his own. 'It didn't take her long to write to me,' he murmured. He stopped, then, finding it not quiet enough, went another twenty paces or so. 'Dear friend,' wrote Madame Maze, 'I have been expecting you every day as usual. Are you perhaps ill? I shall be waiting to hear from you that all is well.' He put the letter back in his pocket. He felt relieved. 'It's curious,' he thought, 'to feel relieved when I'm not really.' He began to walk, with his head down, as he did in his flat, without knowing where he was going. He talked to himself. 'What a pantomine! She didn't want the money. But I

103

only had to have it for her to want it. People are extraordinary. Her husband could keep the money for twenty years and she found that quite natural. The money just did not exist for her any longer. Ah, but in the last forty-eight hours everything has changed. Now she thinks the money is important. Just think, I've got it. Everything is different.' At a certain point, in order to avoid a main street, he turned round. 'I shall be waiting to hear from you.' He had been repeating the phrase for the past minute. 'She's only waiting to hear from me!' he said, still speaking aloud. 'So she isn't asking me to go and see her. She grants that I may not come any more, that I may be ill, without for a moment contemplating coming to help me.' He felt afraid. He was obliged to stop. Whenever he became aware of some unexpected show of hostility, he immediately found it impossible to move. He had to wait, without stirring, until hope came to life again. A few moments later he was on his way up to the flat again.

'Emily,' he called.

His overcoat was unbuttoned, his hat over his eyes. He had not even put down his shopping-bag.

'Emily,' he called again.

She appeared with a suspicious expression on her face.

'You are an idiot,' he said.

She did not answer. There comes a time when insults, because they are hurled haphazardly, lose their power to wound. She had good reason for being constantly on her guard. One never knew what Maurice would do. The day before she had looked after him. He had seemed grateful. A night had passed and he was insulting her.

'You are an idiot.'

She shrugged impatiently. Lesca pulled off his overcoat with such force that one of the sleeves turned inside out. He dumped it on the bed.

'Listen to me,' he said. 'Listen to me, I have something to say to you. You don't know how to get along in life. It's ludicrous. Everyone can get along, but not you. Why don't you answer?'

'You talk all the time,' she said calmly.

'And now I've had enough. I don't want to get angry. I've been angry too much already. It makes me ill. Do what you

104

like. Live wretchedly. Let your son waste his time. And to think that you used to maintain you would do anything on earth for your son.'

'I'm an idiot,' said Emily.

'You don't understand anything.'

'Perhaps you would like me to ask you for some money, now that you've got some.'

'Ask me?'

'Yes, you,' said Emily.

'You are even more stupid that I thought. So you think I would give you some.'

'Oh, I know quite well you wouldn't give me any. That's why I shall never ask you for anything.'

'Ah, that's why!' cried Lesca.

'Yes, and for other reasons.'

'And if I were to give you some! After all, you are my sister. It would be quite natural.'

'I should refuse.'

'But I have no intention of giving you any. Oh, no! I know only too well how difficult it is to get.'

He stopped, out of breath. Emily made as if to spit several times.

'You are sickening . . . you respect nothing . . . and anyway I've had enough . . . be quiet . . . I beg you, be quiet . . .'

'I haven't finished,' continued Lesca, 'I haven't finished, my dear Emily.'

He went up to her and tried to take her hands. She pushed him away roughly.

'What's the matter?' he enquired gently. 'You don't want to believe in my affection. You don't realize that it's because I love you that I'm insisting that you do something. I should like to see you happy, in your own home, near your son.'

'Don't begin another pantomine!'

'You see . . . you don't understand me. When I speak to you from the heart, you reply as if I were a stranger. I want you to be happy, Emily, I know you could be, if you wanted, and that's why I am upset. You seem to be accepting your lot. I should like you to do something. Why do you mistrust everything I say to you?'

105

He tried once again to take his sister's hands. She pushed him away even more roughly. He was taken aback for a moment. Then he went on in the same tender and disillusioned tone.

'Whatever you do, Emily, you will never put me off. As long as I live, I shall try to make you happy.'

'Good heavens, how you talk!'

'Yes, I shall do everything in my power. I tell you again, Emily, that if you wanted, you could find some money. You are not very young or very pretty. But neither am I and I find some.'

'What do you mean?'

'You could be attractive. You are fifty-four, aren't you? If you weren't always lying on your bed, if you were charming, lively and agreeable, if you wore a few small pieces of jewellery to give you a bit of sparkle – I could lend you some jewellery – great changes might take place in your life. Old people often need women like you to keep them company. Once you had a place, you could make yourself indispensable. All sorts of extraordinary things have happened like that. If you wanted, I could introduce you to Professor Peix, for example. He's old, he's a widower, he's very susceptible to flattery, he's not as rich as he says, but he is by no means poor. You could coax him and end up by winning his confidence. You would certainly find a way of getting something from him . . .'

While her brother had been speaking, Emily's eyes had not left his face. She had even moved very gradually nearer him to make him think she was allowing herself to be persuaded.

'What a wonderful idea!' she exclaimed.

'And you could ask me for advice.'

'Yes, and you could even come and see me in the evening when he was asleep.'

Lesca began to laugh.

'I'm not joking,' he said.

'Neither am I.'

He took Emily's hands and this time she did not pull them away.

'Aren't you surprised at what I have just said?'

'Oh, not at all.'

'You don't find it extraordinary that a man like me can talk like this?'

106

'Why should I? I'm always hearing you talk like that.'

Lesca pulled down the brim of his hat and put his hands in his trouser pockets.

'Do I look like an adventurer?'

'Not really.'

'I can make other people work and I can give advice. In fact, if our scheme as regards the professor comes off, there's no reason why we shouldn't share. Wait, I'm going to light a cigarette.'

Emily passed her fingertips over her eyes, something she normally never did. She could not bear people who kept touching their faces.

'This is a pathetic conversation,' she said.

Without another word, she went into her own room and closed the door behind her, something else she never did either.

'It's not worth going to the rue Monge,' thought Lesca. He was quite untroubled. The least Madame Maze could do was to wait for a reply. He pondered as he wandered along the embankments by the Louvre and the Tuileries, propelled gently by the warmth of the setting sun on his back. For he had not wanted to stay at home. He wanted to think about Emily and he could not do it except when he was away from her. 'Life would be so simple,' he thought, 'if people didn't build up images of themselves, if they followed their true nature and didn't think themselves obliged to play up to their image. The person has to be ignored. It's just the image that has to be considered. Poor Emily thinks herself a most excellent woman. So then I have to think her a most excellent woman . . . And there we are! Poor Emily.' Lesca watched the Seine flowing ceaselessly towards him and the river would not be the first to grow weary. He felt as if the flesh of his face was sagging and as if the shadows were forming hollows on his features. He was sorry he had not thought of putting on a shiny hard collar. He had forgotten to slick back his hair under his hat. A lock of hair was escaping over his forehead, giving him an ambiguous look, as paws would have done. He also thought: 'It's extraordinary how people believe everything we tell them and form judgments of us so rapidly. If we tell them the opposite of what we think, they believe us. But if, later on, we tell them the truth, they don't believe us. Emily and her virtue! Madame Maze and her unselfishness! But what about me?'

He went home at about six o'clock. Emily was not in the first room. He did not even find the courage to call her. He hung up his coat and hat. He went and glanced out of the window. He felt tired. All at once he seemed to come across the explanation for his condition. There was just one thing he had meant to think about, which he had wanted to think about and had had to leave in obscurity because of the morning's upset. It was himself, his own life. He needed to see it again, suddenly, unexpectedly, in order to attempt to understand its meaning. Had he been a man without a heart, a dishonest man? Of course, his actions would not gain anything by being dragged out of the fog of ordinary life. The hope of some sort of personal advantage lay behind every one of them. But at least he had never willingly done anything wicked. And suddenly, when he had just sat down in the leather armchair, near the window, he realized that he had never been wicked, or dishonest, or cruel, or selfish, but that he had simply been frivolous. He had been frivolous. That was what he was, that was what he always had been, frivolous.

'Emily,' he called.

She appeared at once. He had given her some dreadful advice. He thought she would never speak to him again. Well, no, she had not changed. She was knitting exactly as before. Had she forgotten everything? Or did she attach no importance to his words?

'Emily, do you know what I am?'

'No.'

'I am a frivolous man.'

'I don't think so,' she replied.

She sat down by the table. He had also wanted to ask her: 'Emily, what do you think about this morning?' But she was so calm there was no point in it at present. She would merely have looked at him in astonishment. She would not have remembered a thing. And then she would have made an angry movement, as usual, 'this pantomime again!'

Lesca said to her:

'I'm tired. When you go down, would you be kind enough to bring me my milk?'

She answered with an amiability that surprised him. It was as if it was not he who had been maltreating her, but she who had been in the wrong by taking him seriously.

'Thank you,' he said.

'Oh, there's no need, Maurice.'

'You know,' he went on, 'I really believe what I said to you this morning. You mustn't let scruples get in your way. If an opportunity offers, take advantage of it, take the money and make your escape. Don't worry about me. I shall always manage. I shall say I haven't got your address and don't know where you have gone.'

'Yes, yes, I'll think about it,' she said.

He realized that above all she wanted to avoid a scene. He took care not to mention his disappointment. For a moment he almost lost his temper, but he felt he would not be strong enough and would have to give way very quickly. When she had gone, he threw himself back in the armchair and put his feet up on another. 'Yes,' he murmured, 'it's true, I'm a frivolous man, frivolous. That's what I have discovered today. I would never have believed it.'

Although he had thrown himself on to his back and all his weight was supported by the back of the chair, he still felt a slight pain, or rather a sort of tickling in his back just behind the pit of his stomach. He stood up, hoping that the movement would make it disappear. That was just how his seizures began, with an insignificant little pain, as if there was something hard, a pebble or perhaps a stone, right in the middle of his body, between the organs or inside one of them. Very slowly, the pain would grow more intense, but imperceptibly, so that he might well believe he was a victim of his own imagination.

Emily came back. He forgot his pain.

'Emily,' he said, 'would it be a bother to you to warm my milk?'

'Not at all,' she replied.

He went and stood near the kitchen door. He watched her as she worked.

'I've brought you an egg too,' she said.

'You shouldn't have bothered, Emily. I don't want anything. But cook it for yourself, since you've bought it.'

'No, thank you. I've got my own.'

He had still forgotten his pain. He was watching what Emily was doing. She had a special way of doing things that touched him. She stopped to think between every movement. When she picked up a bowl, for example, she held it in her hand for a while, seeming not to remember why she had it. When she had filled it with milk, she stopped again, not knowing where to put it. These hesitations brought an expression of tenderness to Lesca's face. In his eyes they did not mean that his sister was absent-minded or lost in thought, but that she was still the simply brought up, old-fashioned girl, and that the hardships which marriage had imposed on her had touched her only superficially. As far as the world was concerned she had grown old, but not for him, her brother. He remembered that he had been fond of her, then that he had forgotten her. Between a man and a woman, that is comprehensible. But between a brother and a sister! What had happened that he had not been able to retain even the smallest fragment of his affection? He remembered the base feelings he had been subject to then. She did not do him enough credit in the eyes of the people whose company he hoped to keep. He could see them again, those people. But how did it happen that later, when he had changed his mind about what he admired, he had not thought of trying to repair the damage he had done? They had already drifted too far apart. And he had not minded . . . 'That's what it is . . . frivolousness,' he thought. Besides, neither had Emily. Nevertheless it seemed that, since they had been so fond of each other, something must have remained, that their shared disappointments ought to have united them again at the first opportunity. But no. They had both followed their own ways, struggling to overcome all the little difficulties of their own lives. That was what Lesca was thinking about as he watched his sister.

'Emily,' he said, 'I'm going to sit down. You'll bring me the milk?'

110

She nodded. As soon as he had sat down, he felt the pain again. It seemed stronger. Was it going to increase still further, as it had done that day in the restaurant when he had had to be carried into the proprietors' living quarters? Before he sat down to table he had felt just such a pain as the present one. He had had his lunch, thinking that the warmth would do him good as usual, and all of a sudden he had been pierced through with a sword. It had lasted for three hours. He had called for help, he had begged for an anaesthetic. Would that pain come back? He had other things to think about besides what he could feel in his heart. He had his health to think about, his milk, his peace of mind.

'Maurice, your milk has boiled, you can come and get it.'

For a moment he almost said: 'What! Aren't you going to bring it to me?' He stood up. He had forgotten his pain again.

'Emily,' he said a few minutes later.

'What do you want now?'

He was not surprised that his sister's kindly mood had disappeared already. He was not angry with her. He knew that these changes were modelled on his own.

'I'm in pain,' he said.

Exactly at that moment he realized that he really was in pain.

She did not reply.

'What's the matter with you?' he cried suddenly.

Anger had suddenly gone to his head, like vapour from alcohol catching fire.

She gazed at him with exaggerated astonishment.

He stood up. His anger had died down as quickly as it had risen. Emily was still looking at him with the same astonishment which seemed to belong not to her but to all reasonable people on earth. He did not worry about the look. He walked about with very small, very rapid steps. He could feel the pain but it was not strong enough to monopolize his attention. He was thinking about other things.

'Emily, you must forgive me,' he said. 'I get these fits of temper. You see, there are times when everything disgusts me, when I have the feeling I shall never get out of this miserable condition, except by dying. Of course I would give you a bit of money if you wanted.'

He glanced at her covertly to see what effect this had on her.

111

She appeared not to have heard the word money.

'I, give you money!' he cried. 'I ought not to joke like that. It isn't kind. All I can do is give you a ring, a little ring that isn't worth much.'

He pulled one out of his waistcoat pocket, put it on the end of one of his fingers and made it sparkle. Emily had a horror of strange jewels, as of all concrete manifestations of wealth. She turned her head away.

'This is quite a pretty ring,' said Lesca. 'I can give it to you, if you want.'

'I don't want it,' she answered.

'Why?'

'I don't want anything from you or anyone.'

'That's silly,' said Lesca.

She looked at him in her exaggeratedly astonished way.

'And money?' he asked, pretending to turn away while still keeping his sister in sight.

'Even less.'

He sat down again. Once again he was very calm. It was as if he were keeping an eye on himself and after every outburst felt relieved that he had maintained his self-control.

'Emily,' he said, as if he was speaking of some indifferent matter, 'your attitude is stupid.'

'Why?'

'I repeat, your attitude is stupid. You know very well it is.'

'I don't understand.'

'You understand very well. You are intelligent enough.'

'So I'm intelligent, for the time being.'

'All you have in the world is a son and that son needs money. You come across an opportunity to get some money and you don't see it. You refuse the money I'm offering you.'

'You want to give me money!' said Emily ironically.

'It's only you acting strangely. And me.'

'You really want to give me something!'

'Come on, take the ring,' he said.

'I don't want any ring.'

'And money?'

Again he pretended to look behind him.

'You want to give me money!' cried Emily.

112

Lesca turned to his sister, looking her straight in the eyes. His gaze was so penetrating, so deep, so painful, that she blinked. He gripped her wrists.

'Look at me,' he said.

She poked her chin forward and opened her eyes as wide as she could.

'I, give you money!' said Lesca. 'You always fall for it! Where would I get it from then, this money?'

As he spoke, he pulled out his wallet, then put it back hastily with the grotesque action of a man, or rather an actor, who, wanting to prove his innocence, realizes that he is doing the opposite.

'You have some money,' said Emily.

'Of course.'

'Why do you say you haven't any?'

'Of course I've got money if I offered you some,' said Lesca.

She began to laugh. He copied her.

'You may well offer, it's not difficult when you know the offer won't be accepted.'

'In any case, I've never offered you anything seriously,' he said.

She became grave again.

'You are absurd,' she said.

'And you are poor and always will be.'

She shrugged her shoulders. Suddenly he bent double. He immediately got out of the armchair and took a few steps, still bent double. As the pain stayed just as intense and remained exactly the same whatever position he adopted, he straightened up, then sat down again, then stood up, then bent in two. He did not know what to do with himself. Whether he stayed still or moved about, the effect was the same.

'Emily,' he said, despite the rigidity of his cheeks, 'I'm in pain, I'm in pain. It's true, this time . . . what should I do?'

'Go to bed,' she said.

She removed the clothes that were lying on the bed and extricated the pillow. He let himself fall on to the bed, hoping that the fall would ease him. He turned on to his stomach, then on to his side. He tried to raise himself by leaning on one arm. Perhaps some awkward movement would do him good. He let himself fall back. His head banged against the wall. He was still moaning.

Emily looked at him but dared not go near him. Although he frightened her, she was not at all certain that he was really in pain.

'Rub my back,' he said with difficulty.

She took off his jacket.

'No, no, telephone,' he said. 'I must have an injection. It's unbearable. I can't stand it any longer. Emily . . . Emily . . .'

'It will pass,' she said.

He had hidden his face in the pillow. He could be heard gasping for breath.

'Have a very hot drink,' she said.

She went into the kitchen. There, as she had done a little while earlier, she stopped for a moment by the stove, seeming not to know how to begin. At last she lit the gas. Then again, before she put the water on to heat, she gazed at the flames for a long time. Lesca was crying out now. She seemed not to hear him. It was her brother suffering like that! But was he really suffering? She had not even thought of lighting both rows of flames. This fat, sick old man was her brother, the young brother of whom she had been so fond! She went to the door to look at him. She saw him writhing on the bed. He had changed, but she had not. She was still slim, still ready to be fired with enthusiasm. She had not wanted to grow old.

Shortly afterwards she brought him a cup of herb tea. It was hard work making her brother drink it. All of a sudden he stopped moving. He was lying on his back. There was no cushion raising his head. His eyes were wide open.

'Are you feeling better?' she asked.

His lips scarcely moved. For a few seconds he had been free of pain. It had vanished so strangely that he was afraid that even the vibration of a single word in his throat might make it come back.

Emily sat on a chair close beside him.

'Yes, you are getting better,' she said gently, stroking her brother's hand with a circular movement.

'I think . . . I'm . . . getting better,' he said, making three attempts at it as if, before he spoke, he had collected the words in his mouth.

'I can see you are,' she said.

He wanted to move. She stopped him. As he was bathed in sweat, she went to find some blankets and covered him up.

'The pain is extraordinary,' he said.

'Where does it come from?'

'I don't know. Nobody knows. Poisoning. I think it's poisoning.'

A few hours later he went to bed. He was so happy to be free of pain that he would have been content never to move again, or eat, or drink, or read, or see anyone, content to live quite motionless, in semi-obscurity, far from everything. It did not take him long to fall asleep. When he woke up, he had no idea what time it was.

'Emily,' he called.

He wanted to see her, to try to find out what effect the attack had had on her. He remembered that in the restaurant, when he had been carried into the first floor flat, he had also wondered what people had been thinking about him. Had they looked on his as a condemned man? He had been well aware of the sight he had presented. He remembered asking for a clothes-brush, as if he had merely slipped, and saying as he left that the most eminent doctors did not think his case serious, that that sort of thing occurred very rarely and had never had any importance. Then he remembered the grave illness that was at the root of the troubles he was now suffering. Things had happened in the same way as they had just recently. Throughout his life he had thought it quite likely that he would one day fall ill. He had imagined that then everyone would close ranks around him. And when he had realized that, although he was seriously ill, he had had to make as many efforts as a healthy man to get people to look after him, and take care of him, he had been extremely surprised. Nobody had done anything. Emily had not done anything. There was no point in relying on anyone but himself and his own defences. Once again he had come through. He did not stir in order not to lose the benefits of his victory.

'Emily,' he called softly.

She appeared.

'Where have you put my jacket?'

'Don't worry. It's beside you, on the chair, and so is your wallet.'

A strange look of disappointment passed over Lesca's face.

'I'm not worried. Nothing is important to me any more, Emily.'

'Yes,' said Emily.

Lesca felt that the attack he had just had gave too much weight to his words. He was annoyed about it. He began to smile, but the attack gave too much weight to the smile as well.

'I'm surprised to see you,' he said. 'I'm very surprised. When I woke up, I saw a light in your room. But I thought you had gone.'

She looked at her brother maliciously.

'Why are you looking at me like that?' asked Lesca. 'It would have been quite natural.'

'I see what you are driving at,' said Emily.

'I shouldn't have held it against you. I should have quite understood. I should even have approved your action in my heart of hearts. Of course, you have become used to certain things here. It's hard to break away from things you are used to. But you would be so much better off in a flat of your own. You could bring your son there. He is such a sensitive boy. And I should live as I did before you came.'

While he was speaking in this affectionate manner, she showed signs of greater and greater exasperation.

'I should have understood very well,' continued Lesca. 'It's not much of a life living with a man like me, in poverty, with a man who has these dreadful attacks. There are two possibilities: either I am exaggerating my illness, which is not funny, or I am not exaggerating it and will die, and that's not funny either. It would have been better to take advantage of the opportunity and leave.'

'What opportunity?' asked Emily grimly.

'The opportunity you had just now. It was an opportunity. I should not have noticed anything. And when I was myself again I should have been faced with a *fait accompli*.'

'You wouldn't even have noticed there was anything missing.'

Lesca appeared not to hear.

116

'I should have waited for you, then I should have realized that you had gone. Then I should have resumed my former life. I should have changed the bed. I should have moved a few objects about a bit . . .'

'Oh, I understand perfectly,' said Emily. 'But you are deceiving yourself. When I go, I shan't take a thing with me.'

Lesca pulled himself half up and stayed leaning on his elbow even though he was immediately overcome by fatigue.

'What!' he cried, 'You would have taken something with you!'

'I've just told you I wouldn't give you that satisfaction.'

'That satisfaction! What?'

His elbow slipped. He fell on to the pillow, afraid of pulling a muscle.

'Let's talk about something else,' he said. 'It's always after scenes of this sort that I get my attacks.'

When people are ill, they only have to have nobody in their field of vision to think they are on their own, or at least to pretend to think so. With his eyes on the ceiling, he murmured:

'Satisfaction, satisfaction . . . So that's what she calls it!'

Lesca stayed in bed all day. He felt well. He could have got up, especially as the weather was beautiful, changed, shaved and gone for a little walk, but it seemed to him that he would not get back to shelter again. Every time Emily passed through the room he turned away his head. He never spoke to her. He was angry with her but he did not know why. Yet she had been very attentive during his attack. He remembered now that she had stroked his hand. This memory made him somewhat uncomfortable and so did the memory of having thanked Emily. 'Thank you,' he had said. He felt a shiver, or rather a kind of nervous tremor from one shoulder to the other. It was as if, when he was in dire distress, he had eaten a piece of bread given him by the very man who had caused his distress. He was ashamed of himself. 'People are always ashamed after they have been ill,' he thought to justify himself. He still dared not look at Emily. Several times she asked him if he needed anything. He answered 'no' and at the same time made a curt movement of the head. From time to time he thought about Madame Maze. She now seemed to him a worry and a hindrance. What riled

117

him most was the feeling that she had not been straight with him, that she had made him do what she really wanted. She must have made inquiries. It seemed to him that she had been doing and thinking things she did not tell him about, that she became different as soon as he had gone, that she knew very well what she was aiming at and was far more practical than she was willing to allow him to believe. And then, a frightful thing, she must be jealous of him. She had guessed he was pursuing an elevated end. She was trying to stop him attaining it. She was the only one allowed to have finer feelings. Now she realized that he had them too, she was showing her true nature. So there was no need to be astonished that she had written a letter like that. What meanness! That she should write a letter like that after forty-eight hours, when she had been making a great play of being unselfish for years, certainly made one think.

From time to time Lesca dozed off. As the day went by, he felt more and more weary. Toss and turn as he might, he could see nothing but grimacing faces. Emily had given up asking him questions. It seemed to him that she had never crossed and recrossed the room so frequently. She got on his nerves. Now he could watch her without the risk of her being aware of it. She held herself upright. She was not afraid to plant her feet on the ground. She looked as if she wanted to show him that she was in good health. But perhaps Lesca was inclined to see things in a black light.

He stayed in bed for another whole day. 'When it's over, nobody cares about you.' But as he lowered his eyes whenever Emily went by and reviled her inwardly whenever she came near him, that was quite natural. She was well aware of it. 'The older men get, the more like one another they become. People no longer make distinctions, unless they knew you before you were old. One can be rich or not, it's all one fundamentally. You have to make up your mind to it. You must not take offence or expect too much. And then, if you are ill as well! It's then that you reap what you've sown, as the saying goes. It would have been better to make friends when the going was good, to make people like you. Afterwards, people remember that you did not try to help them. And so they don't try to help you. You shouldn't have thought yourself so strong. What a drama!'

It was almost night. Emily had not put on the light. She was old too. But it is not the same thing for women. They age so soon. Lights from cars were being thrown on to the ceiling. Lesca closed his eyes. It stung them as reading did to see the lights crossing, shattering and merging. Occasionally, a large restful light spread slowly from one wall to the other. Oh, if only he had lived in a flat that was huge, clean, warm and luxurious! He would have got up, had a bath, shaved. And if he had had some fine clothes, soft and well cut . . . He would have been another man. He would have felt free. A maid would have served his dinner respectfully, at a great white table in a large, well-lit room. He would have read the illustrated papers and illustrated books. Then it would have been easy not to think about himself any more and to get better.

'Emily,' he called.

'I'm coming,' she said. 'Well, how are you?'

'Much better. But I shan't get up. If you wouldn't mind, get me a seventy-centimes egg. Take care they don't give you a sixty-centimes one.'

Emily went out. It was not completely dark. Lights were flashing over the ceiling in all directions. Lesca kept his eyes closed. His face was at rest, in spite of his prickly beard, his stiff hair and his open collar which showed a grimy undergarment. He thought about Professor Peix. Perhaps it would have been polite to get in touch with him. Of course, it meant going up four flights of stairs. But it would have been a sign of trust and respect to ask him for his help. He had to be understood. One should not always think that people hated being asked for things. On the contrary, they liked it. It did not do to be like Emily. It did not do to be for ever saying: 'Oh, I shan't ask for a thing. I'm a respectable woman!' On the contrary, you ought to ask and people were grateful for it. Those who did not appreciate this truth finished up like Emily, completely alone. He at least had never been afraid to ask. It was true that he was alone all the same.

In the morning he got up at eight o'clock. He did not feel so well. He had hardly slept. Suddenly there was a knock

119

at the door. He went pale, then asked Emily to open it. It was a registered letter from Madame Maze. 'I am extremely surprised at your silence,' she wrote. 'You understand that there is cause for anxiety. Perhaps you did not get my first letter. I am therefore sending you this one by registered post. I shall expect a reply from you today.'

For a while Lesca remained motionless. His lips kept on opening and closing. 'What a woman!' he said clearly from time to time. He began to walk up and down. 'So soon . . . so soon . . .' he said.

'Emily, read this letter.'

She took it fearfully and read it.

'I don't know what it's about,' she said. 'I don't know the woman. Anyway, don't tell me anything. I don't want to know anything.'

'You don't understand?'

'No.'

'Oh, well, you see where not knowing what you want leads.'

'Where?'

'Would you want to be one of those crazy women who imagine all their lives that they have something they must defend? Until they are twenty-five it's their virginity. They defend their virginity and, after they have lost it, well, they find something else. You always look as if you think someone is going to harm you.'

'Me?'

'Yes, you.'

He softened.

'It's not at all important,' he said.

He let himself drop into the armchair. Now and again he glanced covertly at his sister. His head and hands were beginning to tremble.

'Emily.'

She turned towards him. He looked up at her beseechingly.

'Are you feeling ill again?'

'No, no,' he said. 'I don't know where I am.'

'What?'

'Where are we?' he asked, apparently not recognizing the room.

'You shouldn't have got up,' said Emily.

Lesca closed his eyes. When he opened them again, Emily was tying a shoe-lace which must have come undone. He did not see her tying the lace, he saw her leaning forward, her head bent towards the ground. It often happened that he took some ordinary movement for a movement caused by pain. Then he would be seized with terror, until he had recognized what the movement was. This confusion was the real reason why he never had a meal with Emily. To begin with, no doubt because she was very tense and nervous, she had several times choked as she ate. He had been so frightened that afterwards, if even the slightest change took place in her face, he had been seized with the same fear.

'Emily,' he said.

Emily straightened up. He sighed so deeply that his chest seemed to move forward. There was nothing the matter with Emily. She had tied her shoe-lace. For a few minutes he rejoiced in the feeling of well-being that floods over us when we have avoided an accident.

'Emily,' he said.

'What?'

'Listen to me, Emily. I can't possibly tell you what is going on inside me. But I must talk to you. My idea is to make you happy. Why? I don't know. I can't say. I have always had this idea and I have never been able to bring it about. It's very strange. Today I'm wondering if I might be able to. Wouldn't it be marvellous?'

Emily was looking at him, her eyes growing wider and wider with astonishment.

'I don't need anything myself,' he went on. 'I shall never need anything again. That's why I laugh when I get a letter like that one. That woman really is unbelievably stupid. She's frightened, you hear, Emily, she's frightened. She's frightened of me. She doesn't trust me. How can one make such mistakes? It's extraordinary how people can change so quickly, how little it takes for them to . . . but this is of no interest to you, Emily. My idea is more interesting. To make you happy. You. Why? I don't know. It's just my idea.'

'I'm not unhappy,' said Emily.

121

'You will be free, Emily. You will no longer be dependent on anyone. I ought to have acted sooner. You will leave. I shall give you everything. I have never done anything at the right time. Ideas come to me too late. It's not that I don't care.'

'I don't want anything,' said Emily stiffly.

Lesca drew several rapid breaths. For a little while he said nothing.

'Life is so wonderful, Emily, wonderful, wonderful, wonderful. It seems to me that I should be infinitely grateful to anyone who spoke to me as I am speaking to you.'

He went up to his sister and, as if he was speaking to an accomplice in a public place, bent towards her ear.

'You will take everything, and leave, and go and live wherever you like, and you will be happy, happy, happy . . .'

He lowered his voice still further.

'You must be happy, Emily. I'm going to make an admission, I've only just found the courage to do it. I can't be happy myself if you are not. This admission perhaps comes too late, like everything else. You must be happy, Emily. Then I shall be happy too.'

Emily had drawn back. She was thinking: 'Maurice is ill. He's going to have an attack. What's to be done?'

'All you have to do is leave when I'm not here, if my presence embarrasses you,' said Lesca. 'It might well embarrass you. I can understand that. But I'm going out soon. All you have to do is take the opportunity.'

Still looking at her, he began to walk on his toes.

'There will be no need for you to walk like this,' he said.

He banged his heel on the floor.

'You can make a noise,' he went on. 'It won't matter at all.'

He was covered with sweat. He wiped his forehead but the sweat went on running down his neck. His collar was damp. All of a sudden he dropped on to a chair.

'Emily,' he cried.

'What's the matter?' she asked.

He was panting. His eyes were pleading.

'Emily, come here, come here. Do something for me. I need some peace. Come, come.'

She obeyed uneasily. He took her hand, put it on his forehead and then let go of it. Emily withdrew it at once.

'Emily,' he said, 'leave your hand there. I need the contact. It'll be better soon.'

She put her hand back on Lesca's forehead, but turned away her head.

'Don't bother,' he said.

Before he stood up, he turned round, in order to support himself on the back of the chair. He took a few steps, looked at himself in a small mirror and smoothed his hair.

'Emily,' he said, suddenly calm, 'it's agreed, isn't it?'

'What?'

He seemed surprised.

'I have understood absolutely nothing,' she said. 'Besides, I don't think there is anything to understand.'

A silence settled between brother and sister.

'Have I been play-acting again?' asked Lesca at last.

'Yes, of course.'

He turned his back abruptly on Emily, then faced her once again.

'It's shameful,' he cried.

'What's shameful?' said Emily.

'You've a funny way of thanking me.'

'I've nothing to thank you for.'

'Poor woman!' said Lesca.

'There's no need to pity me,' said Emily.

'Be quiet,' cried Lesca.

He was no longer in control of himself. He kept on gesticulating with both hands. All of a sudden, he became still.

'Emily,' he cried, 'I've had enough. I'm going. You hear, I'm going. You'll never see me again. I'll never set a foot here again. It's over. My patience is limited. So is my kindness. I'm going.'

He seized his overcoat from the hook, turned it as he put it on, then made for the door. But just as he was about to open it, he came back again.

'No, I'm not going,' he said.

'Do what you like,' said Emily.

'Yes, I will do what I like. I'm not going. I'm staying.'

He began to laugh.

'Emily,' he said in a changed voice, 'I wanted to frighten you.'

'You didn't make me afraid.'

'I wanted to frighten you by saying that I was staying,' he said, raising his voice again.

'You don't know what you're saying. If you're really ill, you'll have another attack.'

'But I'm leaving.'

Emily did not utter a word.

'Shall I go or shall I stay?' asked Lesca.

'I don't know,' said Emily.

'I'll stay,' he said.

'That's fine.'

'No, Emily. I'm going. I'm going and I shall never come back, you hear, never, never. Do you understand?'

This time he actually did go out. On the second floor, he stopped. With a hand on the rail, he turned to one of the doors. 'Poor dog,' he said, 'you whine, but I whine too.' As soon as he found himself out in the rue de Rivoli, the noise, bustle and light overwhelmed him. He had no idea of the time. As he was cowed by the Tuileries, the Concorde and the Champs-Elysées, he had turned right. He did not know where he was going. Suddenly he realized that he was in the place de la Bastille and that it was twenty to twelve. He sat on a bench, near the metro station. A child gestured rudely at him from a carriage. It upset him. It occurred to him that he could have gone to the rue Monge. At midday Madame Maze would be making her lunch. There was no risk of being seen through the window. But what use would it have been? He had wandered around the bookshop twice already. Should he go back a third time? It was becoming a bad habit. No, he would never have believed that Madame Maze would behave in such a way towards him. What pettiness! How was it possible to appear so changed? Of course, he had seemed very different too. Madame Maze's attitude was only a reply to that. 'That is precisely what I don't like,' he murmured, 'people who return word for word and deed for deed.' For more than an hour he strolled backwards and forwards along the fence beside the track of the metro. He was not waiting for anyone, he was there by chance and he could not make up his mind to leave. He was now thinking about Emily. She at least did not reply. She at least would not stoop to defend herself. She was a hard woman, stern and defenceless. He did not know why she had always provoked him to pity. 'Why?' he wondered. She would not accept advice. She had always done what she wanted. 'It's true that everyone arouses pity in somebody. Don't I arouse pity in certain people too, in Peix, his son-in-law and his daughter, for example, and perhaps even in people I don't know but who know me?'

The door of the building where he lived had never before seemed so big and heavy when it was closed. It had never occurred to him that it might not open. He rang the bell. It was getting on for one o'clock in the morning. He rang again. At last he heard the mechanism click five or six times in succession, quite pointlessly, as the door had opened at the first click. As he was passing the lodge, he stopped. There was a crack of light between the curtains. He knocked gently on the glass. There was no answer. 'Lesca,' he said. 'Is my sister still here?' There was silence all round him. He waited for a moment longer, not daring to speak more loudly. Then he began to climb the stairs. He was so tired that he came to a halt every two or three steps. He had spent the whole day wandering about. He had even gone to the rue Monge. He had fallen asleep in a cinema. He had taken two hours to write a letter which he had afterwards torn up. Now he was returning home exhausted and anxious. What had happened in his absence? Perhaps Emily had gone. Since he had said he would not be coming back, perhaps she had thought: 'What's the point of staying?' He opened the door noiselessly. He had only taken a step or two when he caught the sound of Emily's slight snore. Walking on tip-toe, he went into his sister's room. He turned the light-switch very gradually. All of a sudden the light came on. He looked at Emily. He was surprised. She was sleeping with her arms raised, curved above her head in childlike abandon, which formed a contrast with the deep hollows of her armpits between the fleshless tendons. He put out the light. There was no hurry. It took him ten minutes or so to reach his bed, being extremely careful not to make a sound. He had not always been so respectful of other people's sleep. But that night Emily's seemed to him to be sacred. He sat down on his bed without removing his overcoat. For more than an hour he stayed like that without moving. From time to time he said 'Emily', in a low voice, in such a way that she would have heard him if she had been awake. Suddenly he remembered the letter he had received the day before. A wave of shock ran through him. The day had passed and he had not managed to get a reply to Madame Maze. He thought: 'There are some people who always think people are making fun of them.' Madame Maze was one of those. 'It's a bit much,' she must be saying to herself. 'He didn't even have the politeness to reply.' As if it could be a question of manners at this moment! he thought: 'How petty these people are who begin to hate you just because their pride has been hurt! I ought to have gone to see her, written to her, brought her flowers, chocolates – and then, oh! everything would have been different.'

Once he was in bed, Lesca tried hard to keep his eyes open. He did not want to wake Emily, but neither did he want to be asleep when she woke up. He wanted to be there. He wanted to surprise her. He did not want her to surprise him. Whenever she turned over or heaved an inexplicable sigh, he sat up in order to be able to hear better what happened next, because he felt half-deaf when he was lying down. But nothing else happened and he let himself fall back. Even if he dropped off in spite of himself, he still kept his attention strained on the next room. In the morning he woke up with a start. He got out of bed without realizing what he was doing, then stood still. Was Emily awake? Had he stupidly spoilt everything at the last minute? Fortunately not, for she was still asleep, even more deeply than in the middle of the night. He knew that she slept in just that way towards the end. She never woke up peacefully (like a child opening its eyes) but as if she was emerging from a nightmare. He dressed silently. Then he sat down again and waited. Suddenly the sound of Emily's breathing no longer reached him and he heard instead noises which seemed delightful to him, the sound of lips parting, and so on.

'Emily,' said Lesca.

126

She did not answer. She was pretending to be asleep. She thought that because her eyes were still closed nobody would notice. She did not suspect that her brother knew she was awake.

'Emily, it's pointless.'

He went into her room. She had opened her eyes.

'I should like to speak to you,' he said.

She sat bolt upright in spite of the hollow in the mattress. Although her hair was very disordered, she did not put her hand to it.

'All right,' she said. 'I'll get up.'

He went back into his own room. He was dressed but had not washed or tidied himself at all. He sat down at his desk. He looked without interest at the odds and ends scattered about in front of him. He never picked them up or stroked them. Then he stood up. Emily had just joined him.

'What! Are you still there?' said Lesca, as if he had not known that his sister was in the next room.

'Didn't you call me?' said Emily.

'I didn't know you were there,' Lesca went on.

'What sort of story is that?' said Emily.

She went back into her own room. Lesca followed her. His eyelids felt as if they were being stretched because they weighed so heavily on his eyes. His lips and nostrils were dry. 'I ought to have put some water on my face,' he thought.

Emily was smoothing the covers over her bed, embarrassed by the crumpled hollow where she had been lying.

'You had told me you would not be coming back,' said Lesca, 'that you were going away and I would never see you again.'

Emily turned abruptly.

'You were the one who wasn't going to come back,' she said like a shot.

'I?' said Lesca, 'I, not come back to my own place? Why? And where would I have gone?'

'Don't start again,' said Emily. 'I know how you carry on. When you haven't done something, you say that it's other people who haven't done it.'

'Emily, yesterday you said to me: "I'm going away and I shan't come back." Am I dreaming?'

'I don't want to have an argument with you,' said Emily. 'In the first place, it's too early.'

'Answer me.'

'That's enough, Maurice. You know very well you were the one who wasn't going to come back.'

'Me?'

'Don't pretend to be surprised.'

'I even woke the concierge when I came in yesterday evening to ask if you were still here.'

Emily shrugged her shoulders.

'You can ask him,' said Lesca.

'There's no point,' said Emily.

Lesca had been making a show of humility, craning forward, shoulders bowed and hands outstretched. All of a sudden, he changed. He was trembling with rage. It was as if a ray of light was flashing over his face, moving rapidly from place to place.

'I'll turn you out,' he shouted.

Emily took two steps backwards, still facing her brother.

'What an extraordinary thing to say!' she said.

'Did you understand? I'll turn you out. You can go straight away. I've had enough. What are you waiting for?'

'Very well, very well,' said Emily, in the sort of tone that is adopted for the benefit of some imaginary spectator by people whose violence is only temporary.

'I'll turn you out. Then you can laugh,' said Lesca, who had noticed the irony and had become even angrier.

Emily realized that this time there was something more serious than usual in her brother's words.

'Do you really mean what you're saying?' she asked.

'Go, go, at once. I . . . I . . .'

Lesca had got himself into such a state that Emily gave up speaking to him.

'That's all right,' she said, turning her back on him.

'I'll turn you out,' shouted Lesca once more.

Emily turned round again. Until that moment she had thought that this burst of rage was no different from earlier ones and would be of no consequence. But when she saw her brother with his mouth all drawn over to one side, she was suddenly frightened.

'You must go immediately,' he cried. 'I don't know how I've been able to put up with you here for so long. A dead weight. It's outrageous. Incapable of budging. Well, you'll budge now. Hurry up, go on, hurry up.'

'Don't worry, I will budge, as you say,' said Emily, feeling anger sweeping over her too.

'What are you waiting for?' cried Lesca.

Emily went into her room. She put a chair next to the wardrobe and took down the case that was on top of it.

'But if you go,' said Lesca, 'you must take everything, everything that belongs to you. I don't want to keep anything.'

'I haven't so many things,' said Emily. 'I arrived with one suitcase. I shall leave with one suitcase.'

'You must take everything.'

'Yes.'

'Everything, you hear, everything. I don't want to keep anything.'

Emily opened the wardrobe. The shelves were extremely untidy. She took out her ragged belongings one by one.

'You must take everything.'

'You're beginning to get on my nerves!'

'Everything. Do you understand?'

Lesca had gone so close to his sister that he was getting in her way. She moved.

'Everything. Did you hear? Everything.'

Emily was on her knees. She straightened up.

'Do you want me to go? Yes or no?'

'Yes, at once. So hurry up . . . but don't forget anything.'

'I shan't forget anything,' said Emily.

'You must take everything,' said Lesca. 'Otherwise I shan't let you go. That's clear, isn't it? All the same, you don't want to go back to Bordeaux or Noyon.'

'I shall see what I shall do.'

'You must take everything, that's easy. Then you will be free. You can go where you like. You won't be dependent on anyone. You can make a new life for yourself – a modest one, because there isn't much, in spite of everything. But there's enough. You must take everything, even what does not belong to you. Do you understand what I mean?'

Emily put her case on her bed.

'No,' she said.

'But you do, you understand very well,' said Lesca.

'Oh no I don't. I don't understand at all.'

'You know very well you can't do anything else,' said Lesca.

'I'll take what's mine, that's all,' said Emily.

'And what's mine too.'

Emily angrily threw down a garment she was folding.

'No,' she said.

'But as I'm giving you permission . . .'

'I want nothing from you, nothing, absolutely nothing. I shall never accept anything. You know that very well. Why go on about it?'

Lesca went into the kitchen to drink a glass of water. Instead of going back in to his sister, he walked up and down for a little while in his room. He talked to himself, gesturing as he spoke. What he said was incomprehensible. He was pretending not to know where he was. He halted in front of the main door, as if he believed it was the door of his sister's room.

'Open the door,' he said.

He removed his hand. He had just noticed his feigned mistake.

'Emily,' he said beseechingly. 'You'll never understand me then. You don't realize that I'm only thinking of your good, that if I keep on like this it's because I know the difficulties that are waiting for you. I want you to be happy. Everything would be so easy if you would understand that. You would leave without any fuss. I should be happy to know that you were happy near your son. You could go and live in the Midi, for example, and one day I should come and see you, only if it didn't inconvenience you, of course. For don't think I'm trying to establish rights over you in this way, you know what I mean. I'm not that type. You are free, completely free. If you never want to see me again, I shan't hold it against you, on the contrary. On the contrary! I don't know why I say on the contrary. But it's true. I should be glad not to know what became of you as long as I knew you were not short of anything. There's something between us, Emily, that stops us speaking frankly. It ought not to be so. We were separated for a long time, but we shouldn't forget that we are brother and sister. You are my sister, Emily.

Why get angry the moment I want to do something for you?'

'I'm not angry, Maurice,' said Emily sadly. 'I know very well that you are my brother. When I didn't know where to go, I came to you. I'm sorry, it's stronger than I am, I can't accept anything from you. I am well aware that fundamentally you are acting out of kindness. But I can't. That doesn't mean I have no affection for you. Besides, when I've gone, we shall get along much better, you'll see. It was a good thing you lost your temper. The situation is much clearer now.'

'Oh, Emily, you can't go like that, with nothing,' cried Lesca.

'Oh, of course I can. I'm not as alone as you think. I have friends. You may not know them, but they exist. Don't you believe me?'

'I believe you, Emily. But that ought not to prevent you from taking what I'm giving you.'

'I've told you already, I can't. I couldn't even if I wanted to. Besides, if you have any money, keep it, because you need it as much as I do.'

'Oh, I don't need anything!'

'I assure you, Maurice, there's no point in going on about it.'

'It's for your good, my poor Emily. It was a long hard struggle to get the money and I was only thinking of you. And now I can at last give it to you, you refuse.'

'I'm not refusing, Maurice. I'm simply telling you how things are. I can't, I can't take anything from you. I'm very fond of you. You are my brother. I'm very fond of you, in spite of your faults, but I can't take anything from you.'

She stopped speaking to look deep into Lesca's eyes.

'Don't you think it's better like that?' she went on.

As he was silent, she answered her own question:

'Yes, it is better.'

'And you, do you think it's better?' asked Lesca, who had not heard Emily reply.

'Yes, much better,' she said.

'You think it's better?' said Lesca, with his eyes half-closed.

'You think so too, at heart,' said Emily.

Lesca straightened up abruptly. His eyes were so wide open that some of the little veins that were usually hidden could be seen. Above his nostrils, his nose was pinched. His lower lip was trembling. He gesticulated wildly.

'I, give you money!' he cried. 'You are mad. I was going to give you money! I was speaking seriously! But for what possible reason? What would have happened to me?'

Emily hid her disappointment. She remained calm.

'Don't get excited,' she said, 'I shall very soon be gone.'

'I suppose you thought I was going to let you take everything. But you would have wondered if I was right in the head.'

Emily picked up the garment she had thrown down.

'I'm not mad, Emily,' went on Lesca. 'Don't touch a thing, you hear me. Take what belongs to you, yes, but don't touch what isn't yours.'

'Don't worry, Maurice.'

Lesca withdrew a few paces.

'Stay here,' said Emily. 'I want to make sure you see me pack.'

'Oh, I had no intention of leaving you alone.'

Emily turned to her brother.

'How can you talk to me like that!' she said.

He sat down by her and lit a cigarette. He was trembling even more than before but nevertheless seemed very calm. From time to time, with a movement of the shoulders he pushed up the collar of his jacket and with a movement of the arms he freed his wrists. Emily folded her clothes slowly, putting to one side those she was planning to wear. When she had finished, she asked Lesca to go out. She wanted to change and put what she was wearing into the case. Lesca withdrew without a word. In his room, he lit a fresh cigarette, but was so little aware of what he was doing that he put it on his desk without smoking it. Occasionally he stopped breathing in order to listen to what Emily was doing in the next room. Suddenly the door opened and Emily appeared. She was wearing a black hat, a coat, and gloves, and had a handbag. Her skirt hung straight down, divided into regular folds. Round her neck she had a dark fur fastened by a big steel clasp. To Lesca she looked just like his aunt in Noyon. He was pale. His mouth was filled with a bitter taste such as he had never experienced. Even if he kept his tongue quite still, the taste spread everywhere, even to his lips.

'Emily,' he said.

She was buttoning her gloves without the slightest affectation, as she would have buttoned her gaiters.

'You are ready, Emily,' said Lesca.

'Yes.'

'You're leaving?'

'Yes.'

'You haven't forgotten anything?'

'No.'

Whenever Lesca uttered a word, there remained a space hollowed out between his teeth and his lower lip, giving his face a sorrowful expression. His eye began to quiver. His hands were hanging down but his fingers kept moving slightly without touching one another. Suddenly he advanced on Emily. She drew back. He grasped her wrists, so strongly that she did not even try to free herself.

'Emily,' he said, putting his face close to his sister's.

'What?'

'You shan't go.'

He squeezed her wrists even harder.

'You shan't go,' he went on, 'without taking the money I'm going to give you.'

He had only just spoken these words when he added hastily:

'Be quiet, be quiet, be quiet . . .'

He shook Emily's wrists.

'Do you understand?' he said. 'Do you understand?' She made a movement with her head but it was impossible to grasp its meaning.

'Pay attention, Emily.'

He was breathing with difficulty. Every ten seconds or so now he moved his shoulders as if he was trying to push up the collar of his jacket.

'Look at me,' he said. 'Look at me. This is a man you don't know talking to you. Look at me. The past is dead. This minute is the only one that counts.'

Emily tried to free herself, but without conviction,

'I'm going to give you some money, Emily. Listen. Be quiet. You must take it. Pay attention to what you are going to do.

133

Everything depends on you. Everything, you hear, everything, everything. Pay attention. If you don't take it . . .'

Emily seemed not to hear. She bowed her head, raised it again, turned it left and right, nodding it and shaking it. Her eyes were moving aimlessly.

'You will take the money,' said Lesca.

He was standing very straight. His tic was gone. His lip was back in place.

'I'm going to give you some money,' said Lesca. 'And you will take it.'

'Yes,' said Emily.

For a little while they stayed there, not uttering a word. Lesca had half-closed his eyes. That 'yes' in his sister's mouth had seemed to him marked with infinite gentleness. He appeared to smile.

'And if I kept on starting again,' he said. 'That's what I was doing.'

Before Emily had time to reply, he added:

'No, no, don't worry, Emily. I'm not going to start again.'

Just as Emily was about to leave the flat, he planted himself in the doorway.

'You shan't leave,' he said.

She moved him out of her way. He took her hand and stroked it.

'Are you going?' he asked.

'Yes.'

When the door had closed again, he threw out his chest and held his head high. He stayed like that for a few seconds, then, abruptly, his shoulders slumped. He listened intently. He could hear footsteps on the staircase. 'Stay, Emily,' he said aloud. 'I don't want you to go.' He fell silent because the sound of his voice prevented him from hearing the footsteps. 'Poor Emily, poor Emily.' He fell silent once more. This time he could not hear the footsteps any more. He ran to the window and leaned out. He saw Emily getting into a taxi. What address could she be giving? He remembered that she had said: 'I'm not as alone as you think. I have friends.' He saw the taxi moving off and joining the stream of other vehicles. Soon it was out of sight. He closed the window again. Was the flat empty? He sat down in the leather armchair. Suddenly he shivered. He had just remembered Madame Maze. He had not answered her. He would never answer. What would she do? He wondered about it for a long time. Then his face cleared. He was thinking: 'She won't do anything. It would be so much out of character.'